LOSING TOUCH

SANDRA HUNTER

ONEWORLD

A Oneworld book

First published in North America, Great Britain and
Australia by Oneworld Publications 2014

Copyright © Sandra Hunter, 2014

The moral right of Sandra Hunter to be identified as the
Author of this work has been asserted by her in accordance
with the Copyright, Designs and Patents Act 1988

Paperback ISBN 978-1-78074-382-0
ebook ISBN 978-1-78074-383-7

Printed and bound by CPI Group Ltd, Croydon, UK

The characters and events in this novel are fictitious.
Any similarity to real persons, living or dead, is
coincidental and not intended by the author.

Oneworld Publications
10 Bloomsbury Street
London WC1B 3SR
England

Stay up to date with the latest books,
special offers, and exclusive content from
Oneworld with our monthly newsletter

Sign up on our website
www.oneworld-publications.com

For Maureen Luxton and Hugh Dunton who
opened doors and taught me to walk forward

PART I

A TENDENCY TO FALL

SEPTEMBER 1966

The viewing of the body has started. Arjun breathes in cold chapel air, looks around at his family, the Kulkanis, and friends of Kulkanis, and those married to Kulkanis. The family is large and loud and quarrelsome, but today they are a subdued queue, forming in front of the coffin. Jonti: beloved younger brother; quick with a line to make you laugh, quick-witted answers that found him an architect's job in London, but not quick enough to outpace the disease that took him at thirty-two. Five years younger than Arjun. It is wrong.

An overripe west London September presses damp, sticky heat into the small chapel. Even so, Arjun's hands are cold. His wife, Sunila, sits beside him wearing dark glasses; his son, Murad, is scowling and his daughter, Tarani – what convinced her to wear purple?

He tries a whisper. 'Sunila. Take those off.'

She holds her hand up to her face and edges back, as though he is about to snatch her sunglasses away.

Murad lifts his sad, patient expression. Sunila tucks a handkerchief into the cuff of her black blouse. Look at them – just look. Sunila can't bring herself to wear a sari, claims it doesn't suit her, it's too long, too uncomfortable. *We don't wear that kind of thing here.*

We. How earnestly she has embraced the culture that rejects her. They have lived in Hayes, north London, for twelve years and she longs for the acceptance held out of reach. Her English colleagues at the insurance office ask her opinion on curries. She provides recipes with translations of the difficult Hindi words. They ask if she still speaks Indian. She explains she was brought up speaking English. *How funny – just like us!* Yes, just like them.

Arjun catches Murad's eye and smiles. Murad quickly looks away. The boy clings to his mother, even though he's twelve – an age, surely, when he should be more interested in his friends.

Arjun tries to remember himself at twelve. Back in India, in his younger days, he was a runner, a climber, the first one to find a new route up the side of a mountain, the first to run down from the school to the village in less than thirty minutes. He is startled to find he can remember the feeling of running, feet barely touching the ground, almost flying. Was that really him?

He feels the tears rising. His brother, Jonti, also ran; not as fleet, but determined. Chubby little legs trying to catch up. *Arjun, Arjun, wait for me!* And those legs followed him, growing longer, more muscular, the voice once high-pitched, now yodelling, now dropping a full half-octave deeper than his own. His little brother, who grew up to enjoy the strange language of numbers that conjoined, split apart, writhed together on multiple planes, that translated into shapes that rose and fell like empires, threw out fishing lines across graph paper and disappeared off the edge, reappearing as columns, city blocks, telegraph poles.

Jonti was a genius, they said. He could have been in research, but he settled for an assistant architect's position that allowed him eight-hour days, time for a life with his wife and their two little girls.

Jonti told Arjun, 'We've given up enough, isn't it, just by coming here? I don't want to leave my family for all this nonsense travelling to America and Bahrain and Saudi Arabia. What do I want with this MIT and H2M and AHA? I have enough *aha* in my life as it is.'

Arjun remembers the fuss over Jonti, a Hindu, marrying a Muslim girl. Their mother, the highly respectable Monisha Kulkani, was appalled. A *Muslim*? These days, young people marry whomever they want. He expects Murad will come home one day with some girl in jeans and short, dyed hair, and they will have to smile at her while she makes comments about their food, their *batiks*, their lovely culture.

He glances at Tarani. She is nine. In the old days

she might have been betrothed by now. Some girls were betrothed even earlier. Horrible custom. He shivers.

It hadn't been easy for Jonti. But finally, his mother's and the aunts' hissing slid away before the pragmatism of his father and the uncles. Jonti had a good job and could provide amply for Nawal: let them marry. Nawal's family, high-caste but impoverished, was less accommodating. They disowned her.

Now, Arjun looks over at his poor purple-clad child. He would never disown her, no matter who she decided to marry. Her legs are thin and they curve away from each other. She should wear longer dresses. Tarani has one hip thrown out, her weight on one leg, chewing a fingernail before she notices him and whips the finger out of her mouth.

At the front of the chapel, Nawal is surrounded by a group of women. She cannot bring herself to view the body. Arjun knows he should do something. He stands up to join the queue near the coffin. He will see Jonti for Nawal. It is the least he can do.

Jonti is dead. My brother. Thirty-two. Less than a year from energetic young man to a half-presence inside pyjamas that became too large too quickly, head bobbing to one side as if shaking the motor neurone disease out of one ear.

Arjun tries to breathe more deeply, but the scent of lilies is too strong. The chapel is too small. He is now third in line. Someone should open a door, should hold up Nawal who is going to collapse. Surely there isn't enough air for her: she will faint. It is his turn to step forward, to look into the face of his dead brother.

Suddenly, he is falling. A quick grab at the coffin saves him. They must think he is overcome with grief. He looks at Jonti's calm, empty face. How can he leave his brother in this ridiculous box with satin and pillows? Jonti would be appalled. *What's the use of primping and posing and all when you're dead,* bhai*? Spirit is gone, isn't it? Phut. Up into the air. After you eat the panipuri, only empty paper is there. Let it blow away in the breeze.*

He steps away to make room for the next person and looks around to see Jonti's two little girls, eyes too big, too stark. He gathers both of them in a hug and they hang on. They are too young to lose their father. His eyes are misting when he hears Sunila's voice. 'Arjun?'

He settles the girls back into the pew, manages a smile, and walks back with Sunila trailing him.

Nawal's sister, Haseena, is near. He apologizes to her. 'I'm so sorry. I must have tripped.'

'I've been tripping over everything,' she says. 'I can't judge distance any more. It feels as though I'm in someone else's body.'

She has accurately described what has just happened. For a moment, he felt his body falling without him. The strangest idea. It was just a slip. There are more important things to consider. As Jonti's older brother, he must now take care of Nawal and Haseena. They will need a man's help now, especially in this country.

On his way back to his seat he glances at Nawal. A faint touch of her perfume reaches him. Jonti always bought her Chanel No 5. *The best for the best.* The scent takes him back to when Jonti bought the first tiny bottle.

When they'd arrived in England in 1954, Arjun had gone straight into the RAF at Northolt. He had a job, a uniform and a rigorously disciplined life that was mostly away from home. Meanwhile, Jonti faced the job search head-on, presented his credentials and listened to numerous reasons why he couldn't be hired. He finally found an assistant architect's job in central London. Jonti's route to work took him by tube to Bond Street Station, then a walk along Oxford Street past the imposing bulk of Selfridges to the office in Portman Mews.

Once in a while, schedule permitting, Arjun would take the train to meet him from work. For two years, Jonti had passed and repassed Selfridges without a thought of what might be inside. And then came Nawal's twenty-first birthday in 1956. Arjun and Jonti stood nervously just inside the massive brass and glass front doors. Jonti had wanted to leave.

'Should we even be here? Posh people and all.'

'Jonti, just relax. We're the same as everyone else.'

'Not the same, *bhai.* No other Indians in here, nah? Not even cleaning ladies.'

'It's okay. We'll just buy the perfume and leave.'

'Security will throw us out on our ear. "What are these brown buggers doing in Selfridges?" '

'It's just a financial transaction. Come on.' He had patted Jonti on the back as they stepped up to the counter.

Arjun's throat is aching. *I loved him best.* This is something he has never admitted to anyone. As he sits down, Sunila hisses, 'I hope you realize what you've done. Making a scene like that. Hanging all over the coffin. What were you thinking?'

He doesn't know. For a moment, his body behaved as though it wasn't his. 'We are grieving. Jonti is dead.'

She puts a handkerchief over her mouth and he can see tears trickling out from behind the dark glasses. She whispers. 'It's just that Jonti… It was the same as Mum.' She gasps. 'I miss her.'

It is something, perhaps, that his mother never lived to see her youngest die. Frail and desperately homesick for India, she lived long enough to attend Pavitra's wedding and then succumbed to the same disease as Jonti.

Sunila and Mum must have been close, he supposes, although he never really noticed it. His own relationship with his mother was respectful, formal. Still, Sunila is suffering and he must do something. He moves to put his arm around her.

'Don't touch me. I don't need any of *that*, thank you.'

The children stare ahead, Murad's mouth an exact copy of his mother's. Tarani has her hands tucked under her thighs, her head carefully turned away.

One day, it will be their turn in some chapel like this one. He wonders if Sunila will mourn him like they are mourning Jonti. To mourn, surely, you must also have experienced great joy, and Jonti inspired happiness. Arjun wonders what he inspires in Sunila.

Haseena is hosting the wake, since this is the first time Nawal has been able to get out of bed. Haseena's house has been hung with black crêpe and wreaths. Her touch shimmers behind it all: her gold and cream cushions, the cinnamon sofa, the silver candlesticks. Her house of light is overlaid with the shadows of Jonti's death.

Nawal cannot bring herself to respond to anyone. She is handed around from relative to relative in some sad, fragile game of pass the parcel. He watches how she fails to lift her head as each one embraces her, enfolds her. As each pair of arms surrounds her, she seems to slip further away.

He goes upstairs to the bathroom and squeezes past Sadiq, Haseena's six-year-old son, crouching over a transistor radio. 'These boots are made for walking...' As he is coming down again, he is sure he hears Jonti's voice. It is only one of the children, but the sound of his brother's voice is so persuasive that he turns quickly. The next moment, he is sliding to the bottom of the stairs.

Tarani is watching.

He is up almost immediately.

She looks angry. 'You fell.'

'I tripped.'

'I saw you.' In her eyes he sees the accusation that reaches down and jerks up an unnamed fear. 'I saw you in the chapel, too.'

The others are coming.

'Are you all right, Arjun?'

'Too much wine, Uncle?' One of the cheekier nephews.

'*Arré*. I'll give you a clip.' An irate aunty.

'Come and sit here, Arjun.'

'Have some Love Cake. Haseena made it.'

And Haseena arrives, the soft cloud of her cream chiffon pallu smelling faintly of lemon and mint. 'Come, Arjun. Let me give you some tea.'

He is glad that Sunila isn't close by. How she would bustle and push people away. Her husband, her responsibility. *Did you tie your shoes properly? I've told you. A hanging lace can cause a broken neck.*

Haseena deftly moves with him into the kitchen and brings tea, says nothing about the fall until she sits opposite him at the table. 'Arjun. I am your sister-in-law and we are able to speak with each other.'

'Of course, Haseena. You can say whatever you want.'

'Don't put this off. Go to the doctor.'

'It's nothing. I'm just clumsy today.'

'But what if, Arjun? Please?' She looks down. 'I don't know if Nawal told you. The first time Jonti fell was when he was getting out of the shower. He laughed about it.' Arjun can imagine his brother. *Clumsy fool, nah?*

He nods.

Before she can say more, Sunila arrives. 'What happened? Are you hurt? Murad said you fell downstairs.'

Haseena immediately gets up. '*Didi*, can I bring you tea?'

'Not for me, thanks.' Sunila turns her attention back to Arjun.

'I'll go and see if anyone else wants tea.' Haseena picks up a tray on her way out.

'Didi! Why can't she drop all this Hindi-bindi business?'

Arjun says nothing.

'And what was she saying? How long were you in here with her?'

'Sunila, she gave me tea. I slipped, that's all.'

'Their family is so conniving. You know how she caught those husbands of hers.'

'Haseena's marriages were arranged.'

'I know what I know. Both of them dead, just like that.' Sunila pauses for breath. 'How did you slip on the stairs? Is the carpet loose?'

'Possibly. I don't know. Anyway, I'm fine. No damage done.' He smiles at her. Sunila is only worried. She doesn't know how to show love any other way. 'Come. Let's go back to the others.'

At the other end of the dining room near the French doors, he sees Tarani. She has a slightly blank look that means she's trying to remember something. Instantly he knows. She's trying to remember exactly how he fell. The fear comes back. Surely they're all making something of nothing.

He smiles at her to show he's okay. She doesn't smile back.

2

COMPLICATIONS

OCTOBER 1967

'She's my sister-in-law. I should be invited too. She needs a woman's support now that Jonti…' Sunila jangles a percussion of cutlery into the sink.

Jonti. It's only been a year, but his brother's name can still make him catch his breath. Arjun smooths the spoons into the divider and picks apart the forks and knives. He folds a pan holder patterned with one large thistle leaf.

'Haseena did invite you. But you'd already made plans with Pavitra.' He riffles through the clutter of coasters. Jonti would have had some joke to make Sunila laugh. 'You could still come. Why not invite Pavitra along?'

'To *her* house? I have some sense of decency.'

'You want to come, or you don't want to come? What do you want, Sunila?'

'Look at her. Living high on the hog.'

He is disgusted by the peculiar American phrase. 'Please don't speak like that.'

'It's not like I'm calling Haseena a pig, isn't it? Only the way she lives. Egyptian sheets and washing machine and dryer and what-all.' Sunila begins to hammer the pots and pans into a cupboard. 'All I know is, she can't stay married.'

Haseena's first husband died from an overdose of sleeping tablets. The second husband was old when he married Haseena and died happy, six years later, having managed to leave her with a son. But Arjun can see that Sunila finds it too much of a coincidence. She is practically Wildean about it. *Losing one husband is unfortunate; losing two husbands…* Perhaps she thinks Haseena is cursed with the Evil Eye.

Despite Sunila's love of arguing with the unlucky Mormons who occasionally knock at the door, and her ability to quote long passages from the Bible in a staccato monotone, she is sensitive to an older, darker faith. Her right cheek tingles whenever something bad is going to happen. Arjun is tired of hearing premonitions of terror and destruction that are confirmed when she turns on the television. *See? War in the Congo. I told you. My cheek doesn't lie.*

He might dismiss the Evil Eye, but Sunila's evangelical beliefs have hammered their way into Arjun. He wasn't much of a Hindu anyway and he wanted some kind of religious education for the children. Sunila firmly settled them into a local Seventh-day Adventist church. At first, he stuck to the periphery of church activities, reluctant to be involved. And, for his evident Christian humility, he was elected head deacon.

The shock of being propelled into church meetings and board duties gave way to a feeling of being placed somewhere. The satisfying predictability of his weekend duties has led him to recognize that he does have a god of sorts. As he follows his quiet routine of setting out chairs, neatly stacking the weekly programmes, wiping a duster over the pulpit, his god appears in the early-morning light from the high windows across the clean linoleum floor of the church. Arjun's god seems content to potter about the pews and smile gently from the sidelines. Arjun is aware that his god would be found wanting by Sunila's god. He wonders if everyone's gods get together to swap notes. Some might be shy, others more convivial. Sunila's god, the bossy one, would make all the jokes while everyone else would politely listen. He catches himself. Surely it's blasphemous to think of the Christian God in the plural?

The door is flung open. Tarani bursting with injustice: 'Mum, it's not *fair*. He's got my tranny. It's *mine*.'

'Stop all this screeching. Speak slowly and calmly.' The interruption makes Arjun irritated.

'But it's *mine*. And he won't *give* it to me.'

'Now, now. I'm sure Murad will give it back.' Sunila tries to calm her.

'Leave this to me, Sunila. All this nonsense about a transistor radio. We should never have bought it in the first place.'

'It was a Christmas present, Arjun.'

'It's not fair. I *hate* him.' Tarani's crying twists her thin face.

'Be quiet!' Arjun, always surprised at how Tarani can make him lose his temper so quickly.

Sunila tries to joke Tarani out of her sulk. 'You know you always exaggerate.'

'Sunila, stop pandering to her.'

'What's all this pandering-shandering?'

'You're interfering with—'

'*I* interfere? I was just talking to her—'

'It's not *fair*.'

Arjun turns and slaps Tarani's face. Her mouth drops open.

'You brought it on yourself. Now go upstairs.'

Tarani rushes upstairs. He can hear her sobbing. So dramatic at such a young age. It is Sunila's fault. He had the situation well under control and then she ruined everything.

'She'll get over it.' He lifts his chin away from the shirt collar.

Sunila begins to wash a couple of mugs in the sink. Let her sulk. He has a bus to catch. 'I'll be back this afternoon. Give my love to Pavitra.' He keeps his voice level as he exits the kitchen.

He buttons up his coat and clears his throat. Discipline is essential for children. Anyway, it was only a tap. She'll be fine by tonight.

Outside, the cold air lifts him away from the needlings of stress. His shoulders relax, his walking pace picks up and he breathes into the quiet of the street.

A neighbourhood of identical semi-detached houses: some of them strain for a sense of separate identity with their shutters painted green, yellow or maroon, the front doors stained pine or teak. A breeze ripples the airy fields of TV antennae as he turns to walk up a tree-lined road. An iron fence runs for about an eighth of a mile, enclosing Heinz Laboratories, the buildings set back in their park and screened by tall stands of trees. They need a lot of privacy for whatever fearful ketchup experiments they conduct.

The brisk pace calms him and he arrives at the bus stop feeling cheerful. It is a clear October morning. The birches cling on to summer, while beneath the chestnut trees the handspan leaves change colour and the beeches are skirted with red and purple patchwork.

The bus comes quickly and Arjun settles into a window seat, watching as the road pulls away from lingering fields, gradually gathers small parades of shops, housing estates, a comprehensive school, an eruption of traffic lights and finally narrows its brows as it ploughs into the coriander-mint chutney and *achari* mutton smells of Little India, Southall, where the shops run their wares right out onto the pavement. Women in saris and shalwars flip dupattas and pallus over determined shoulders to do battle with shopkeepers.

A young girl in a shalwar khameez slips into the seat in front of him. How sweet she looks in her shalwar, something that Tarani would never wear. The girl settles her dupatta scarf over her head and turns to look out of the window. She softly hums a tune, nodding her head.

The bus slows to a crawl as the men and their women and their daughters and sons and the perpetually astonished babies, and the pavement-gazing bent-backed old men, one hand behind their backs, the other holding a black cane that stabs at the road in front of them, cross in front and behind until the bus is a small boat carried along through an endlessly parting and closing sea.

The young girl hums and taps pink-frosted fingernails against the window. A woman sitting in front of the girl turns around and stares. The girl doesn't notice, and Arjun is pleased. Let the child sing.

The bus settles into a low gear, drifts along, gentled into a different time, and another tune drifts into Arjun's mind. He is transported back to India, to the boarding-school Christmas party. Loops of green and red and blue paper chains wreathe the hall, the twenty-foot tree, heavy with tinsel and lights, bending slightly to the right as if listening to the music. He'd been dancing with Anju Padiyar, turning solemnly round and round to this very waltz.

The soft shuffle of feet across the floorboards, a teacher winding up the gramophone one more time. Anju is a pretty girl. If only she were Lorna.

Anju jerks his hand. 'Am I invisible, then?'

'What? Oh. No. I'm sorry.' He smiles at Anju, as Lorna is swept past him by a tall Marati boy, who drags her about as if she were a mop.

'I suppose you'd rather be dancing with *her*.' Anju tosses her dense mass of dark curls. Anju has round eyes, an upturned nose, a perfectly round rosebud mouth. Arjun knows there are at least fifteen boys who would love to be in his place.

'Who else is in the room when you are, er, in the room?'

Anju rolls her eyes. 'Is that the best you can do?'

'It's a beautiful night, isn't it?'

'It's boring. You haven't said *anything* about my dress. Or my hair.' The curl-toss. 'It took me *hours* to get ready.'

She could be wearing a sheet for all he knows. He and Lorna never talk about such trivia. They share secrets: he hates his father, she hates her sister. He hates the captain of the cricket team, she hates that Anglo-Indian Bonnie Deefholts and her long brown hair. They both adore chum-chum, Branston Pickle and library period. She is reading Byron. He is reading *Biggles*. She scolds him for his juvenile tastes. He mocks her love of the romantic poets. Even so, when she is lost among the cantos, he gazes at her wavy dark hair, far more beautiful than Bonnie Deefholts'. He loves how her right eyebrow twitches slightly when she finds something especially beautiful. It is a signal that he must reimmerse himself in his own book, since she will look up to read him a couplet. For this he must look slightly bored, indicating that he is busy reading.

Arjun starts. The conductor is calling out, 'Ealing Broadway'. This is his stop. What nonsense, dreaming over memories. He might have ended up in Shepherd's Bush. As he steps down onto the pavement, his right leg buckles and he is thrown against the metal bus-stop pole. He grabs at it, managing to stop himself from falling. His right leg won't straighten properly, won't respond. People stream past, averting their faces as though he's done something particularly offensive.

A man in a cloth cap and gabardine raincoat stops. 'Are you all right? Had a bit of a tumble there.'

'No, no. I'm fine, thank you. It's just clumsiness. I was getting off the bus.' His embarrassed smile pleads for the man to move on, but he stays.

'Nearly fell base over apex off the tube the other day. Whole army of chaps shoving to get off.' The man has clear blue eyes and a neat salt-and-pepper moustache. 'Sometimes wonder where common courtesy has gone to, these days. It wouldn't hurt for people to slow down a bit, get off the bus like civilized human beings instead of a torrent of lemmings.'

Arjun is momentarily distracted by the image. 'Yes. We do tend to rush about.' Almost without realizing it, he's adopted the man's speech pattern. 'No reason for it, really.'

'Absolutely right.' The man narrows his eyes. 'What regiment are you?'

Arjun realizes he's talking to an old war vet. 'Not the army. Air Force.'

'Ah. Fly boy, eh?' The man laughs. 'My son wants to join up. Told him to keep his feet on the ground.'

Arjun clears his throat. 'I was in the medical corps. Nursing.'

'Capital. Yes. Knew you were a services man.'

Still holding onto the bus stop, his coat rumpled and his leg only just beginning to take its weight again, Arjun knows he cannot possibly look the part.

The man leans in a little. 'Shoes. Always know a man by his shoes.'

Arjun looks down. His highly polished black shoes gleam in the weak mid-morning sun. He glances at the man's shoes. Brown brogues, perforated with the signature pattern, also highly polished.

'Well, I'd best be on my way. Nice talking to you.' The man touches his hat.

Arjun finds his right leg is able to take his weight and he nods. 'Good day to you.'

He stops in front of a shop window to check his clothing. Everything is normal. His forehead feels tender from the collision with the pole. He wipes his face with his handkerchief. No blood. Just a bruise, then.

He walks carefully, but his leg now responds perfectly. How thoughtful of the man to stop and speak to him, to give him enough time to recover, to deflect the curious attention of passers-by. People are so kind.

He tries a more brisk pace and the leg is perfectly all right, as though nothing just happened to make the left leg have to brace against the sudden loss of the right leg. He felt nothing except the lurch of the unexpected. Will it happen again, in front of Haseena?

He walks along the tree-lined street. The houses are more spacious, the gardens much larger. No children tear up and down on bikes or scooters. There is a sense of peace and dignity, the kind of England he read about while he was in India. He relaxes into his usual stride, enjoying the sheer physical pleasure of walking. The fall was nothing; just a small irregularity. He turns left into the familiar cul-de-sac and rings the doorbell at number twenty-two.

He hears thumping feet and a high voice. 'Uncle!' Haseena opens the door, and seven-year-old Sadiq flings himself at Arjun.

'Let Uncle come in.' Haseena hugs Arjun. 'Arjun, so lovely to see you.'

Arjun lifts Sadiq for a hug. 'How big you are, Sadiq. You'll have to carry me.'

Sadiq struggles to get down. 'I can do it, Uncle.' He wraps his arms around Arjun's legs and struggles to lift. 'See? I did it.'

'Are you going to be a weightlifter?'

Sadiq considers. 'I might.'

Haseena stares at Arjun. 'Your forehead — oh, Arjun — what happened?'

'It's nothing. Just an accident.'

'Did someone hit you, Uncle?'

'*Goonda.* Your uncle isn't a prize fighter.'

'*I'm* going to be a prize fighter. Muhammad Ali. Float like a bee.' Sadiq flaps his arms and jumps.

'Go and play while I take care of Uncle.'

'Okay.' Sadiq cheerfully rushes off. 'Don't each lunch without me.'

'I'll call you.'

'Because it's my favourite chicken.'

'I know. Now go.'

'*Fa*-vour-ite *chi*-cken-oo.' Rapid thudding up the stairs.

Haseena peers at Arjun's forehead. She smells of lavender. 'Look at this thing. It's the size of an egg. Come, let me put something on it.'

'It's all right, Haseena. Really. I'm fine.'

Haseena hesitates. 'Tea?'

'Now, that's a good idea.' He follows her into the kitchen and sits at the round table next to the window looking out onto the garden. 'I like this view. You've done a lovely job with your borders. The lavender looks so healthy.'

'I had to cut it back. It was taking over the lawn. I've been making little sachets to put with the towels and sheets in the airing cupboard. I could send some home with you for Sunila.'

Arjun imagines the smell of lavender perfuming the bedroom. But Sunila would be suspicious of any gift coming from Haseena, especially something as intimate as lavender for sheets.

'Nawal and I thought we might sell these. Just to make a little money. But who would buy?' Haseena laughs.

Arjun taps the table with one finger. 'Show me.'

While Haseena steps out, Arjun stares out of her window onto the garden. The blooming lavender is an otherworldly mist, and it wouldn't surprise him to see a fox or a rabbit peering between the bushes. What does surprise him is the sudden throbbing in his head. Perhaps it's a delayed reaction.

Haseena returns with a glass of water and hands him two Panadol. 'These will help.'

He takes the tablets while she moves around, collecting the tea things.

She hesitates. 'Arjun, what happened, really?'

'I was getting off the bus. My right leg. It just gave way.'

'*Bhai*, please go to the hospital for tests.' She pours his tea.

'You make such lovely tea, Haseena. Real tea leaves, not like this teabag business.'

She hands over the lavender sachet, pale green muslin, laced with a lavender ribbon.

'This is beautiful, Haseena. I can see these flying off the shelves.'

'Arjun?' She sits down. 'I've seen this in Pakistan. The leg goes suddenly and then the person falls. Just now and then, nothing to really worry about. Then it becomes more frequent. Then the child… my small cousin had it. She died. Lots of children do. But it happens to a lot of adults, too.'

He smooths the sachet's ribbon. 'I'm sorry about your cousin.'

'But probably for the best. What kind of life is it for a child to sit in a wheelchair and watch others run about?'

'So sad. Poor little thing.' He shakes his head.

Haseena is crumbling her biscuit. Both Haseena and Nawal have the same profile, the same pale skin, the same pretty fingers. Jonti always joked that Nawal had been short-sighted and only agreed to marry him because she couldn't see him properly. *How could she want some blackie like me?*

He clears his throat. 'So, how is Nawal?'

Haseena's hands become still. 'They always did things together, she and Jonti.' She laughs. 'They did this bird-call thing in the house. If they were in different rooms and she wanted him, she'd call "cheep" and he'd reply "cheep-cheep". Sunila said it drove her mad.' She smiles. 'But even if they were a bit crazy, at least they were crazy together.'

She fills her cup and holds the tiny two-cup teapot. 'The lavender sachets are the first thing Nawal's shown an interest in. She comes over. We make sachets and drink tea. So far, it's nothing stronger than tea!'

He smiles, then leans forward and gently takes the teapot from her, holds it in both hands. 'Haseena, you are such a good sister to Nawal.'

She reaches across the table. He looks down at her open palm as though someone has handed him something precious to hold. He tenderly places the teapot in her hand. For a moment she looks at it, then back at him. Her face opens into a smile, and then she begins laughing. Seeing what he has done, he also begins to laugh.

'Really, Haseena. What a clumsy idiot I am. You give me your hand and I give you a teapot.'

'It is also a gift. God moves in mysterious ways.' She opens the door and calls Sadiq.

Sadiq bounces into the kitchen. 'Mum? You know my school lunch, right? Well, Aysha keeps eating *all* my *biscuits*.'

'Aysha is the new girlfriend,' Haseena explains. 'The old girlfriend was last week.'

Sadiq plonks himself on a chair. 'I mean, I offered her *one* but she took them *all*.' His round eyes are astonished.

'It's good to share. Come. Eat.' Haseena serves Sadiq some rice and curried chicken.

Over lunch, Haseena tells Arjun that she and Nawal are arranging a party for family and friends to sell the sachets and other small handmade things. Nawal, she says, could sell the shah his own jewels.

Sadiq asks to leave the table and goes off singing, 'Silence is golden, but my eyes still see'. Haseena and Arjun finish eating and Arjun pushes his chair back.

'Excellent cooking, Haseena. First rate.'

Haseena pulls a face. 'You sound like you're reviewing the troops and I am a kitchen cook.'

He laughs. 'But a *superior* kitchen cook.' He stands up. 'You sit. I'll clear the dishes. I'm an excellent bottle-washer.' It is an effort to stand. He has eaten much more than he usually does at home.

Haseena follows him into the kitchen, sits on a stool and watches while he piles the dishes on the counter next to the sink, fills the sink with hot water and adds a squirt of Fairy Liquid. He starts with the plates, washing and rinsing. She picks up a tea towel. It is peaceful: the soft clop of soapy water, the musical jingle as he rinses the spoons and forks, the clean clack of plate to plate, dish to dish, as Haseena dries and stacks.

'Jonti loved washing up. He said his favourite thing was to have his hands in hot soapy water.' Haseena rubs at a fork with her tea towel. 'And then you'd come back to find him dreaming out of the window. All the dirty dishes still piled up and Nawal comes in and throws her hands up.'

Arjun does the Indian head wobble. 'Okay, okay, sweetie. I'm *so* sorry. Just this minute I'm doing them, isn't it?'

'That's exactly like him!' Haseena, laughing, wipes down the counter.

He dries his hands and looks at the satisfying arrangement of clean crockery on the table. Haseena hangs up the damp towel and moves to put the plates away. Arjun puts out a hand.

She looks at him, puzzled. '*Bhai?*'

He can't explain how he is moved by the neat pile of plates and bowls, the stack of four pans, the gleaming prongs of the whisk, the sheer orderliness, so different from Sunila maniacally slamming everything away as hurriedly as possible. But here, on the kitchen table, is the result of all the work they have done, something lovely and harmonious.

He picks up the pans. 'Just tell me where to put these.'

It is time to go. He'd better not stay longer, even though it would be so comfortable to sit and doze in one of Haseena's large armchairs.

Sadiq comes tumbling downstairs to throw himself at Arjun for a goodbye hug. Haseena hugs him, too.

Arjun tweaks Sadiq's nose. 'It was lovely to see you. Now, you take care of your mother, all right?'

'Arjun, please, you'll follow up with the doctor?'

'Yes.' He smiles at Haseena.

'And let me know?'

'I will.' He turns at the bottom of the path to wave.

'Can I come to your house, Uncle?' Sadiq wriggles as Haseena tugs his arm. 'But Mum, I haven't seen Murad and Tarani for *ages*. Please?'

Arjun calls back, 'Of course you can come, Sadiq. I'll check with Aunty and we'll arrange it.'

'Thank you, Arjun.' Haseena waves while Sadiq does his jubilation dance.

Arjun walks back along the streets to the main road. What a sweet, unaffected boy Sadiq is. If only Tarani and Murad could be more natural. Tarani, especially, is so self-conscious. And Murad. What could have made him so uncommunicative, so distant? Arjun sighs.

Just after Southall, the bus brakes at a request stop. Suddenly the smell of boiled fish overwhelms the memory of Haseena's chicken curry as a tall woman sits next to him. She stares down at him and sniffs audibly, turning her head away.

He hadn't expected the English to be so childish.

'Just ignorance, isn't it?' Jonti, shrugging. 'No more rude than they were in India. Get this, boy. Hurry up, boy.

Jaldi, jaldi.' Jonti's high-pitched version of a British accent. 'Anyone who goes around in a pith helmet and shorts with long socks has no right to make fun of anyone else.'

They were brothers. Surely some of that magic has rubbed off on Arjun? Surely it's possible to love Sunila the way Jonti loved Nawal, to come home with real anticipation? She is wearing a simple but attractive shalwar, her face softens and she looks like the pretty young girl he'd courted in Bombay. She's happy to see him. The scenario grates to a halt since it's impossible to imagine Sunila either in a shalwar or looking happy to see him.

He listens to his body as he gets off the bus, but his leg is fine. On an impulse, he takes the path through the Big Field, breathing in the afternoon cocktail of cold leaves, wet grass, smoke from a bonfire. Four small boys bundle across the grass, frantically aiming kicks at a fast-flying football. The ball bounces off a tree and rolls nearby. Without thinking, Arjun steps off the path, fields the ball and shoots it back. The scrimmage is soon rushing in the opposite direction, the ball leading the struggle of muddy knees and elbows. He watches them go, imagining the excitement of this moment, being in the middle of the pack, the fast breathing, the fleeting second when foot connects with ball.

He wonders when *this moment* deserted him. From one Arjun, always urging his little brother to *come on, catch up*, he grew into another Arjun who led his family overseas to England, to another who developed a respected medical expertise. He substituted accounting for RAF nursing so that the children's schooling wouldn't be interrupted. Now he is yet another Arjun who nervously monitors his own walking. When did the forward rush change into the hesitant step?

He knows what Haseena was talking about. He, too, saw it in India: the leg collapsing underneath the walker, the pitching forward, the look of absolute surprise. It is hard to see that this may be him. *I have a condition. I have an illness. I am dying from...* One thing is certain: if he mentions his self-diagnosis of spinal muscular atrophy to the doctor, it will be dismissed. *You heard of this where? Oh. India. Well. We don't need to worry about that.*

He will go to the hospital. He will submit to their tests, their secrecy, their whispering. The most important thing is not to worry Sunila or the children. They mustn't know. He must stay calm. Suddenly he feels his breath quicken. Will he be like Jonti? Will it be fast? Nawal took care of Jonti so lovingly. Arjun cannot expect that of Sunila. Would she put him in a nursing home? He can't imagine what it would be like to sit in a wheelchair: never to be able to kick a football, run for the bus, play squash. What kind of a life would that be?

There's no point in dwelling on the negative. His step is easy, strong. All the muscles are sending the right messages to his brain. He breathes in deeply, walks quickly and rehearses the scene with the little football boys. It will entertain Sunila.

3

MESSAGES MISLAID

NOVEMBER 1968

In the neighbour's garden, a winter thrush huddles high up in a bare sycamore tree. Short, blunt grass. Cold morning air. Outside, the weather fluctuates, the garden changes, but, in her kitchen, Sunila's feet are planted on well-scrubbed linoleum. The dishes are washed, dried and put away. The refrigerator is organized. The cupboards have food and cooking equipment in neat rows and stacks. Everything is in its place. This is England.

Today, England is chilly. Winter is dreadful, but there is something fascinating about the stillness, the pitiless weight of the cold. It is one of those grey-and-white days where your breath puffs ahead of you. A few days of this, and then the temperature will drop another ten degrees. November in Middlesex.

The phone rings. Pavitra talks so rapidly that it is difficult to make out the words. 'He – he—' She is sobbing. She tries again and Sunila, at first sympathetic, has to bite the inside of her cheek. If only Pavi could hear herself, she would laugh too.

'Suni, he—' She gives up and weeps.

Sunila shakes as she tries to contain herself. Finally she gasps.

Pavitra manages a full sentence. 'Suni, are you all right?'

'If only you could hear yourself, Pavi. He – he – he—' Sunila laughs aloud.

A nervous giggle, then her sister-in-law says, 'I sound like a monkey!'

'Or one of those comedians on television.'

They laugh together, neither able to speak for some moments. The laughter dwindles, they sigh and Pavitra says, 'I like Morecambe and Wise.'

'Me too. Remember that sketch? The one where he puts his foot out from behind the curtain and keeps putting and putting—'

'And the leg is ten feet long!'

They scream again and Sunila sinks onto the stool so she can laugh more comfortably. She wipes her eyes. 'So funny.'

'And clean, Suni.'

'I only like clean comedy.'

This isn't true. Some of Sunila's happiest memories are from parties with her cousins back in Bombay where the men told naughty stories while the women egged them on.

The Morecambe and Wise joke has reminded her of Arjun's failing leg. He never knows when it will happen. But she does. Her right cheek tingles as she sees him walking, the right leg swinging forward just before it stops. If only the tingling began earlier she could warn Arjun, but it's too quick. Anyway, he would think her a fool, telling him that his leg was about to go. Better not to say anything. At least she can make sure she's there so he doesn't fall.

He doesn't want to hear about this, or almost anything else she has to say. He doesn't want to hear about her day at the office, her frustrations with the kids, her ideas about the shelving space in the kitchen, the food mixer that would allow her to make bread. Sometimes he gets angry. *You're just a low-class woman from a low-class background. You'll never change.* She struggles to be a better-class person, like Arjun wants. Jesus has helped her: He is the answer to all the sadness, the disappointment. Even so, sometimes she goes to stand at the bottom of the garden, pretending to tidy up the compost heap, and allows the forbidden thought to come: *divorce.*

She can only whisper it. It's a bad word. Bad people do it. But in the *Woman's Own* magazine at the doctor's office, she read that Elizabeth Taylor had done it. She'd done it so many times that it was just part of her normal routine. Get up, put on face cream, divorce Richard. How daring it sounds, so chic. Sunila practises. Get up, put on Johnson's Baby Lotion, divorce Arjun. *I'll just divorce him and he can take his disapproving face and jump in the lake.* She laughs.

Pavi says, 'What is it, Suni? Why are you laughing?'

'Just thinking about that Morecambe and Wise.'

'Funny fellas.' Pavitra sighs. 'Thank you for listening. I always feel better after talking to you.'

But Sunila has given no advice, offered no help. 'Pavi, how about having lunch? We can go to that Chinese place you were telling me about. The one in Hounslow.'

'King Chow's? Oh, you'll love it, Suni.'

'Let's go on Sunday. How would that be?'

'Are you sure? How about Arjun?'

'He can take care of the children.' Let *him* do something around the house.

Pavi continues, 'The boys are going on a church outing, so I won't have them on Sunday. Thank you, Suni. How sweet you are.'

'No, no. Don't thank me. I'll be so glad to get out of this place.' Sunila hears the words jump out of her mouth. 'You know, just for a change.'

There's a second's hesitation before Pavitra says, 'Yes, a change is always nice.'

'And then you can tell me all about it.'

'Yes.'

Sunila hears the hesitation. 'It'll do you good to get it off your chest. If you'd like. I don't want to press you.'

'You're right, Suni. It's better to talk about these things.'

Sunila will wriggle the truth out of her sister-in-law one way or another. She loves Pavitra, but information is power. If she learns one thing about Pavitra, then it is all right that she has said that she's 'glad to get out of this place'.

Does everyone know the truth about the endless arguments and the times Arjun has hit her? But surely everyone has troubles from time to time. She's seen the bruises on Pavitra's arms and neck. At least her own bruises are easily camouflaged, as though Arjun instinctively knows what long sleeves and skirts can cover.

He says nothing about the plan to meet Pavitra. It is a big favour, even though she spoke so airily about it on the phone. Tarani and Murad are getting together with their cousins, and despite the fact that Arjun will go on about Haseena and Nawal's superior cooking, Sunila feels better about taking a whole day off for herself.

Until six months ago, Arjun always had an excuse to visit Haseena. And then it was have-you-tasted-Haseena's-fish-and-coconut-curry, or why-don't-you-wear-a-shalwar, or Haseena-is-so-elegant-in-a-sari. But in May, just after he'd taken Haseena and Sadiq to Richmond Park, he suddenly went off the boil. When Sunila innocently suggested a family visit to Haseena and Sadiq, Arjun quickly changed the subject. Which meant that he'd had his knuckles rapped. Good. At least the woman has some moral standards and keeps her meddling hands off other people's husbands.

The sick feeling in the stomach starts and Sunila sends up a quick prayer. *Please make Arjun be a good husband. That is, please make him not like Haseena better than me.* She feels ashamed. How childish. She shouldn't be bothering the Lord with these petty concerns.

Sunila gets off the bus and finds Pavitra already waiting outside King Chow's. As they hug, Sunila feels her sister-in-law shivering.

'Cold, Pavi?'

'Just a little.'

'You need a new coat.'

'I'm fine. I should have put on a warmer woolly. Let's go inside.'

It is just noon but the restaurant is already filling up. The two women are led to one of the last window tables. The manager moves between tables, greeting customers. He stops at their table to speak to Pavitra.

'Mrs Owen, so nice to see you again.'

'Mr Chow, this is my sister-in-law, Mrs Kulkani.'

Mr Chow gives a little bow and Sunila nods back at him.

'So, Mrs Owen, you bring me new customer. I give you special surprise.' He smiles and wags a finger at her.

'Please don't go to any trouble.' Pavitra laughs nervously.

'No trouble, Mrs Owen. My pleasure. You choose any dessert you like. On the house.' He beams at both of them and moves on to greet the next customers.

'Such a nice man.' Pavitra tucks her thin coat over the back of her chair.

'I must say, he's a very friendly person.' Sunila carefully folds her coat and puts it on the chair next to her.

'He's like that with all his customers.'

'No wonder it's so popular here. And free dessert, too. What a treat!' Sunila looks out of the window. A real window table. She and Arjun have gone to dinner a few times, but only to Indian restaurants and never at a window table. She is impressed with how clean the Chinese keep their restaurant. No debris on the floor. Tables nicely set. Some of those Indian places could certainly pick up a few tips on hygiene and presentation.

Two of the waiters are Chinese and she watches their smooth, swift movements, their shiny hair, their clean hands. Do they think Hounslow is better than China? She's seen pictures of the watery paddy fields and how they have to work, bent over, for hours. Surely working in a restaurant must be easy after that. And in the evenings, do they pull out their photograph albums and touch the pictures of family members who are left behind? *Home is England,* she repeats to herself. You can choose your home these days. It's the modern thing to do.

The long menu has many choices. Sunila leans forward to whisper across the table. 'Pavi, what should we order?'

'I'll find something nice for us. We'll get a couple of things and we can share.'

Pavi orders chow mein and Kung Pao chicken. Sunila is nervous about eating noodles. What if they fall off her spoon? Will she look a complete idiot in front of everyone?

Pavitra leans forward. 'Suni, the chow mein is very easy to eat. You'll see.' They wait for their tea and Pavitra smiles. 'So nice to get away, isn't it?'

Suni waggles her head, not yes, not no. 'So, Pavi. How are you?'

Pavitra looks down. 'I'm all right, really. I was just feeling a bit run down.'

'Come on, Pavi. You must talk. I mean, we must talk.' Sunila laughs a little.

If nothing is said, the *things* that often lie like dead flowers under their scarves, their nice English blouses, their neat English skirts, do not exist. A few tables away, an English couple are having lunch. Does the woman have flowers beneath her sleeves, too? But English couples are so polite and respectful. It isn't possible to imagine slaps ricocheting across those perfectly pink English cheeks. And the woman's voice, so gentle and sweet-sounding, could never be raised in a screech even if her husband threw a dinner plate at her head. And he wouldn't, because he's English.

Pavitra's napkin, folded and refolded, becomes a hesitant, wavering sculpture. 'It's not *all* his fault, Suni. I try to manage, but he says I waste money.'

'What's wrong with him? You never waste anything!'

Pavi glances around. 'Hush, Suni. We mustn't speak too loud.'

'I'm sorry. I just get so mad at these men. What do they think we do with the money? Spend it on ourselves?' Sunila firmly ignores the memory of buying the cream blouse with the lace jabot that she hid at the back of the wardrobe. It was on sale, after all, and anyway, Arjun had been unpleasant again. At least this time it was just shouting.

'I invited Haseena over. I wanted to make something nice for her. So I made lamb vindaloo. Mike said it was a waste of good meat.'

'What's wrong with a little curried minced meat or vegetables? So selfish of her.'

Pavi smiles and shakes her head. 'Don't be angry with her. It was me who decided to give her lamb. Haseena didn't know, poor thing.'

'Poor Haseena, indeed. She's just taking advantage.' Sunila stares at the happy English couple laughing at each other's attempts to control the slippery noodles.

'He – Mike got angry.'

Sunila looks closely at her sister-in-law. 'Pavi, did he hurt you?'

'No, no.' Pavitra straightens her spoon.

Men and money. It was always men and money. Sunila's father gambled all the family's money away and then died of brain fever. Her mother was stuck bringing up eight children, five of whom died. They could have used some of that money.

'Listen, come to us for a few days. It'll give you a break.'

Pavitra shakes her head. 'It's all right, Suni. I can't really leave the kids with Mike.'

Who could have predicted the way things would go? When Sunila first stepped off the ship at Tilbury Docks, she was uncertain. But the train journey to St Pancras to meet Arjun convinced her that this was the Promised Land. She gazed out of the window, delighted with the fat happy-looking cows. Not like those emaciated creatures roaming around the Bombay streets, defecating everywhere. In England, the cows stood in soft clean grass up to their ankles.

But in Hayes the women looked tired and old. They wore long, beige, ravelling cardigans, smoked cigarettes and some even wore slippers to go to the shops. The children had runny noses and shouted dirty words at her. Some of the men looked straight past her, or if they did look, it was sly. She had arrived in heaven but had been dumped in the wrong part.

A delicate cup and saucer arrives in front of her. The waiter pours the golden tea into each cup and places the tiny silver jug of milk and china bowl of sugar between them.

'Come. Let me serve you some milk.' Sunila lifts the jug and adds a little milk into Pavitra's cup. Into her own cup she adds two lumps of sugar, listening to the soft tinkle of the tiny spoon against the side of the cup.

'Never mind, Pavi. It'll all blow over. Cook something nice for him. Men like that.'

'Yes.' Pavitra rubs her shoulder distractedly. 'I'll make him a good English breakfast. Bacon and eggs. That might do the trick.'

Sunila wrinkles her nose. '*Bay-kin?*' Seventh-day Adventists don't eat pork, and somehow the idea of bacon is even worse than pork chops. Surely it is sinful to prepare bacon, even if you don't eat any. Now Pavi has to cook pig and her soul is in danger. All because of the stupid lamb vindaloo. If only Haseena hadn't been so thoughtless.

'I know. But Mike and the boys love it. I don't mind, really.'

'It's so unfair. We do so much for them. And we don't get anything in return. Nothing turns out the way we want. We just have to face it.'

Pavitra asks, 'Suni? Are you all right?'

Sunila looks down and realizes she has been stirring her tea too vigorously. Some has slopped out into the saucer. 'Oh, how clumsy of me.' She uses a paper napkin to mop up the mess. 'I should have been more careful. Such dainty cups. Not like the big, hulking mugs we have at home.'

Pavitra leans across. 'Any news about, you know, Arjun's tests?'

Sunila breathes in and out. Here it is, out in the open: the trembling reason why she can do no more than whisper the word 'divorce', why she must swallow the insults, endure the slaps, wait out the humiliation of his flirtations. This man, who looked so healthy, is sick. Even if he plays squash three times a week and goes gallivanting after Haseena. He thinks he is so good at hiding his feelings but she, who learned from an early age to stand back and watch, has seen him holding that traitor leg after it buckled once again. She tries to imagine what it is to feel your leg go numb, go missing. She has not been brought up to run away from hardship. *In sickness and in health.* No one is going to help them out in this green and pleasant land where people send their parents off to retirement homes. No one else will take care of Arjun when he can no longer work, when the rest of his body begins to…

'He – well, we don't know—'

Pavitra leans closer and Sunila realizes she and her stupid tears are being shielded from the rest of the customers. She quickly wipes her eyes on the napkin. Takes a sip of tea. Sits up a little.

Pavitra squeezes her hand under the table. 'I keep him in my prayers, Suni. Always.'

'Thank you.'

The waiter brings their chicken and noodles.

'We can say a little prayer now, if you like?'

Sunila nods. No one will notice. It will look like they're saying grace.

She and Pavi bow their heads and Pavi speaks. 'Oh God, our Father, please put Your hand on Arjun. He is a young man, Lord. And he has a family.'

Sunila nods. Even though most people would agree that thirty-nine is definitely middle-aged, in God's eyes Arjun is still a young man.

'Keep him strong so he can take care of Suni and the children. Nevertheless, not our will but Thine be done.'

And Sunila realizes that, young or old, Arjun will not get better. She's heard these prayers many times and been convinced that God would heal. But Bombay-side Aunt Kitty died suffocating, unable to gasp in enough oxygen. And they had prayed through the night for her. Now Arjun, too, is going to die. What is the point, then, of praying at all? She thinks of Arjun as some high-priority folder she's slipped onto the Holy Blotter. What is God doing up there? Is He listening and laughing at their frail human trust? If He can see the sparrow fall, why isn't He doing something about Arjun?

She pushes the thought away as Pavitra demonstrates how easy it is to cut the noodles with the edge of the spoon. Soon they are talking about the children, their jobs, the funny things the comedians say on the television. After their free dessert of lychees and ice cream, they wander along the high street.

There's a sale on at Debenhams, and Sunila persuades Pavi to try on a new coat. It's a beautiful dark blue wool blend that will keep her warm. The coat is fifteen pounds and Pavi obviously likes it, but she takes it off.

'Perhaps another time.'

'Let me buy it for you. Just pay me back when you can.' Sunila doesn't know where this impulse has come from.

'No, Suni. Mike would be so angry if he knew I'd borrowed money from you.'

'But we're family. We always help each other out. It's all right. Mike won't mind.'

Pavitra hesitates. 'But, Suni, I don't get paid for another two weeks. And I have to put aside the housekeeping...'

'That's all right. I don't need the money right now.' Sunila hugs her. 'We'll buy the coat. You can say someone gave it to me, but it didn't fit. We'll cut out the labels and put it in an old plastic bag. He won't know. Men don't notice these things.' She looks into her sister-in-law's worried face. 'He's not going to find out.'

She takes out a ten-pound note and a five-pound note. There's always the chicken in the freezer. She can say that Marks and Spencer had sold out of the black cardigan and skirt she wanted to buy. They were only for work, and her Crimplene skirt and grey wool cardigan are still perfectly fine even though the merino wool jacket would have looked so elegant. Never mind. She can save up and buy them another time.

She watches her sister-in-law put on her new coat, her sweet, delicate face beaming and her long, slender fingers smoothing the fine wool.

'Pavi, you look like the Queen of Hounslow.'

Pavitra twirls around and laughs.

4

INTELLIGENCE NOT AFFECTED

DECEMBER 1969

Arjun grips the steering wheel and clears his throat for the third time. Nothing on the cold, grey A40 helps him out. No incidental-cow-in-field, no hovering lark, no pendulous cranes that young boys are meant to love. Winter colours; faintly frosted fields to left and right fade away into residual mist. The scenery is bald, bland and peculiarly English. If only Sadiq were already here. How is it that a nine-year-old child can get his fifteen-year-old cousin to talk? And Murad doesn't just talk; he becomes energetic, even witty. But there are twenty miles until they meet Haseena, who is dropping Sadiq off for the day's outing to Bekonscot.

Arjun glances at his silent son. He's at what Sunila calls 'the awkward age'. Murad's been at an awkward age since he was ten, speaking less and less. Now he is silent during dinner and at any other time. He does exchange a few words with Tarani.

Today Tarani is with Sunila. *A nice quiet day at home.* They are reorganizing Tarani's room. Tarani had asked for a floor cushion. Why she wants to sit on the floor is baffling to him.

'Just for a change, isn't it? Something pretty to look at. For her to sit on.' Sunila had stood directly in front of the front door.

'She can sit on the bed.'

'It's something special for her. Can't we—'

'I don't have fifteen pounds to throw away on floor cushions.'

Tarani's hoarse voice: 'They're *not* fifteen pounds! They're only a measly—'

Sunila clapped her hands as though she were dusting them off. '*Chuput.* Never mind. Come on.' And the two of them went upstairs.

A year ago, Sunila managed to lose fifteen pounds of housekeeping money. It still makes him angry. How could anyone lose fifteen pounds? Of course, she'd had to pay it back out of her wages. It was a good lesson for her.

Arjun turns the radio on and the strains of that irritating Pachelbel's *Canon* prompt him to ask, 'Can you find something nice for us to listen to?'

Murad tilts his left shoulder as though there's a hidden catch in the request. He looks sideways as a concession to making eye contact and tentatively reaches for the dial.

Achingly slow, he turns the once gilt plastic dial. With the careful precision of a Noh play, Pachelbel edges, note by note, into static that is overlaid with someone shouting about milk, eases back into static, slowly steers into high-pitched honking that eventually morphs into a woman's laughter. Murad's left shoulder relaxes.

The woman continues to honk over the phone while the radio-show host chatters inanely in an Irish accent. Now the man is talking about 'foightin' the flab', some disgusting reference to dieting. The show is obviously for women: house-cleaning entertainment.

Murad is hunched over, trying to close the eighteen-inch distance between himself and the radio. This is rubbish. Can't Murad see that? It's even worse than the other nonsense he and his sister so love, some idiot called Kenny who sings a 'Hello' song to introduce himself instead of a dignified announcement.

Murad hitches himself closer. As the Irish clod says something else, Murad releases a soft snort. Through the long hair, Arjun can see it: turned down at the corners, no teeth showing, but a real smile. Arjun can't remember the last time he saw his son smile. The radio babble continues and the corners of Murad's mouth twitch. Arjun pushes himself back in the seat, rotates his shoulders and settles himself to endure the station for as long as it takes to reach Bekonscot.

Finally, a song. Louis Armstrong singing 'Hello Dolly'. Murad is sitting back, the sullen mask in place.

'You like Louis Armstrong?'

Murad half-shrugs. 'He's okay.'

'This song doesn't do him justice. He's not really a singer. But you should hear him play trumpet. You know "The Five Pennies", the record we have at home? He plays really well. Some people call him "Pops" or "Satchmo". Not very respectful in my opinion. Now, Dizzy Gillespie, he started bebop. Improvisation.' Arjun taps a finger on the wheel. 'Everyone imitated him. And he played with all the big boys. Charlie Parker, Duke Ellington, Earl Hines. Great musicians.'

The Irish voice starts up again and Murad moves slightly forward, just enough to signal that he's no longer listening to Arjun. He probably wasn't listening anyway. Arjun suddenly loathes the Irishman and all these radio voices that can make his son smile, gurgle, snort in ways he no longer can. How easy it was when Murad and Tarani were little. Anything made them laugh. Now they just look at you as though you're speaking Dutch.

He wants to spin the dial, find some Hawkins, Monk, Lionel Hampton; tell Murad, 'Open your ears – *this* is music'. But Murad is half-smiling again, rocking forward as the Irish voice lilts inanities, chats to admirers on the phone, tell his listeners to get up and dance. Arjun realizes he's never seen Murad dance. Is he slow and stealthy, just a little shoulder movement, maybe one hand held out at waist level, fingers curled, the other in his pocket, shifting from foot to foot? Is he, perhaps, one of those who suddenly become animated all over like an electric eel? The idea of Murad dancing like an eel makes him bite the insides of his cheeks. It wouldn't do to laugh at his son.

However, when he finally composes himself enough to look at Murad, to suggest they change the station, the eel image returns and he has to turn a sudden laugh into a cough. He puts the back of one hand to his face in case Murad is looking. And who is he to laugh, when all he can manage is a tentative foxtrot and a shuffling waltz?

Let Murad perform his eel-like gyrations if he wishes. At least he might be happy, although it is difficult to imagine Murad being happy anywhere. Has he ever asked anyone to dance? An approaching roundabout brings Arjun's attention back to the road. He carefully joins the swirl of oncoming traffic, brakes in time to avoid a pushy black van and continues on the A40.

Should he offer Murad advice on asking a girl to dance? How is he to introduce the subject? 'Elusive Butterfly' is now playing and Murad is sitting back with something like his usual scowl. The song grates through its jolly melody and Arjun can't help it.

'Pah.' His usual expression of disgust.

'Mum likes this. Val Doonican.'

Arjun pauses, unsure what to say about Sunila's tastes in music. 'She likes Hawaiian music, too.'

Murad snorts. Arjun can't believe it. A laugh? From his son? Suddenly he feels like he's driving a Jaguar.

'All that twinkly stuff. "Sweet Leilani".' Murad mimes playing a guitar.

Arjun laughs out loud. Murad snorts, Arjun coughs. They sound like two asthmatic old men.

'Well, she likes it. That's what's important.' Arjun is still smiling.

'She says she likes his cardigans.' Murad jerks his chin towards the radio. 'Val Doonican.'

'Don't say that. She'll be knitting us one soon if we're not careful.'

'*I* wouldn't wear it.' A quick head shake to one side to flip the long hair back.

Arjun hugs this small moment of unity with his son, but he doesn't want to appear disloyal to Sunila. 'So, what music do you like these days?'

'Nothing much, really.'

'Come on. I know you listen to the radio, you and your sister.'

'There's Woodstock.' A half-exhalation as though this is a joke Arjun wouldn't understand. 'It's a festival. Lots of bands get together.'

'Ah. And this is in London?'

'It's in America. *Was*. In August. It was in the newspaper. One of my friends brought it in.'

Arjun turns the concept over. Music festival. It sounds beautiful. A celebration of music. In reality, it was probably all this gyrating loud pop music. Just as well it's in America and in the past tense.

Arjun slows down and pulls off the A40 onto Station Road. He glances down, hoping Murad is wearing warm shoes.

They turn onto the long driveway to Bekonscot Model Village and Railway. The silver birches still have a few leaves, trembling, white-rimed. It's been a long time since he brought the kids here to run through the piles of autumn leaves. Today only Murad has grudgingly agreed to come along and keep Sadiq company.

At least there will be some peace. Of the two, he suspects Tarani is the one who causes the fights. Her adolescence is of the cactus variety. One day Tarani announces she loves the Kinks, and the next she hates the Kinks and loves the Rolling Stones. Tarani flings down her statements like gauntlets, hoping for a shocked reaction. The pop groups mean nothing to Arjun. He has even suppressed his disgust and furtively listened to Radio 2 in an attempt to hear some of the songs, but he can't make out what these disco jockeys say or what the songs are about. He has tried to forbid pop music, but he knows the children will find some other way to listen to it.

He pulls up next to Nawal's little dark blue Triumph in the car park. He and Murad get out. A small vibration of nerves as he sees Haseena. These days he can speak to her without feeling the numbing embarrassment that shut him down after that time in Richmond Park, two years ago, when he stupidly tried... Well. That's all past now. They must get on with the business of being family. He uses his hearty voice.

'Good morning, good morning, ladies. No, please don't get out. It's much too cold.'

Nawal rolls the window down. 'Good morning, Arjun, hello Murad.'

Haseena gets out of the car to hug him. He barely touches her; receives her slight embrace. Murad mutters, 'Hello Aunty.'

Haseena hugs Murad, who actually hugs her back. Where did this affectionate side of Murad spring from?

'Murad, I thought of you the other day. Have you seen those blue-and-black-striped bell-bottoms? You'd look very nice in those. Wouldn't he?' She turns to Nawal, who wobbles her head 'yes'.

Murad glances at Arjun and then mutters to his aunt, 'Yeah. They're good. One of my friends got them, the blue ones, down Kensington Market. They've got them in red, too.'

'I saw the red ones in Biba, but I didn't have the nerve to buy them!' Haseena laughs, and Murad releases his quick, embarrassed cough-laugh.

'Maybe you should, Aunty.'

'Oh, listen to him, Arjun. What a charmer!' She turns to Murad. 'We should go, eh? Have lunch and buy some striped trousers together.'

Arjun, surprised by his son's sudden demonstration of social skills, has no idea how to contribute to the striped-trousers conversation. He looks around.

'Where is Sadiq?'

Haseena points to the naked birch trees where Sadiq, in a red bobble hat, is enthusiastically jumping into mouldering piles of leaves. Murad drifts over. Sadiq spots his cousin and joyfully urges him to join in the jumping. Murad stands on a fallen log. Sadiq tries to step up but falls off. Murad lends a stabilizing hand and they walk together along the log. Sadiq shouts with joy as he manages to balance. 'Mum, look at me! I'm flying to the moon!'

'The girls,' Haseena lifts her chin toward Nawal, 'are at a birthday party. So we have a whole morning of freedom. We've been talking about this for days.'

'Lovely.' Arjun looks over at Sadiq. 'What time do you want me to bring him home?'

Haseena turns to Nawal. 'We'll be back at what, one?' Nawal nods.

Arjun nods. 'Let's say one-thirty, just to be safe. Now, sit in the car and roll that window up.' He smiles at Nawal, includes Haseena in the shared smile. 'What film are you going to see?'

'*Butch Somebody and the Breakneck Kid.*' Nawal looks at Haseena.

'Sundance *Kid.*' Haseena is laughing. 'Thank you, Arjun. Sadiq adores his big cousin.'

Sadiq briefly runs over to hug his mother and then goes back to the log. Arjun waves goodbye and the car pulls away. He stamps his feet, even though he is wearing two pairs of socks and his thick walking shoes.

Sadiq is bundled up in a padded coat and a red scarf.

Murad's hands are in his pockets. Arjun now sees that Murad is in jeans, a pink-and-blue flowery shirt and a thin jacket. The loose-knitted maroon scarf that looked promisingly warm in the car is stretched and flung carelessly over one shoulder instead of being nicely tucked around the neck. Despite that, he looks relaxed. Both boys trail over to Arjun as a long green Daimler crunches expensively into the car park.

A woman steps out in white bell-bottom trousers and a long pale-coloured fur coat, followed by a boy, about Sadiq's age, in a suede coat trimmed with white fur. 'It's not *open*, Mummy.'

'It'll be open in a moment, darling.' She turns to the car. 'Morton? Keep the car running. Pokey, you sit inside for a bit.'

'I hate this place. It's never open.' The boy gets back in and slams the door after him. He stares out of the window at Sadiq, who stares back and then tugs at Murad's arm. 'Let's walk on the moon log.' Murad shrugs, and Sadiq runs back to kick through the leaves.

The woman turns to Arjun. 'Well? Is it going to open or not?'

To Arjun's surprise, Murad speaks up. 'The sign says it'll open at ten.'

'I can *see* what the sign says.' She turns her back.

'So why did you ask?'

Arjun is shocked. How could Murad speak like this? He murmurs, '*Murad*.'

She turns and looks Murad up and down. 'Don't you work here?'

'Do we look like we work here?'

'I'm so sorry, madam. We are only waiting for it to open.' Arjun smiles. 'Like you.'

She stares at Arjun and steps back into the Daimler that sits purring on the gravel. Sadiq has come back and looks from Murad to Arjun.

'Murad, what are you doing, talking back to the lady?' Arjun keeps his voice low.

'Toffee-nosed cow.' Murad is openly staring at the Daimler. 'Thinks she's better than everyone, with her big car and her fancy fur coat.'

'I haven't brought you up to be disrespectful.'

'Toffee-nosed cow.' Sadiq gleefully whispers the words.

Murad turns on Arjun. 'If she was Indian, wearing a sari, dragging her kid along by the arm, you wouldn't have been so yes-madam-no-madam, would you?'

Arjun's mouth is open. He is on the point of telling Murad to get back in the car when the ticket office's window opens and the clerk pokes his head out. 'Welcome to Bekonscot Model Village and Railway.' He is a character from any child's story: whiskered face, peaked cap, green uniform with brass buttons. Claps his hands together and releases a steam-cloud of breath. 'Perfect weather for trainspotting!'

Arjun wonders whether they should wait for the woman to get her tickets first, catches his son's expression and steps up to the window. 'One adult, two children, please.'

The man stares at Murad. 'Under fifteen, is he?'

'He's fifteen now.' Arjun tries not to make it a plea.

'Well. Lucky, isn't it? He can still get in as a child.' The whiskers lift in a bright, red, British smile. He stamps the three tickets and pushes them across the counter.

Arjun wants to say something to Murad. The boy can't be allowed to get away with such rudeness. But as they walk through the gate they are presented with the polished miniature world of the English, frozen, improbably, in the 1930s. Huddles of villages, where thatched and stone cottages are crafted with authentic tiny bricks, while the gardens riot in minute gaudy displays. Models of bowler-hatted gents, brollies rolled, newspapers in hands, wait at the stations. A church's stained-glass windows glow while an unseen choir sings drearily. Plaster cows bend endlessly towards grass in fields enclosed with white-painted matchstick fences. In an hour or so, it'll be possible to crouch near a pub and hear the bartender calling, 'What's yours, sir?' above a gentlemanly murmur of voices. And everywhere the steady susurration and clack of tiny wheels as the model trains pass under bridges, over viaducts, through tunnels.

Sadiq stands with his hands clasped together, eyes huge, then follows Murad, who has lost the listless slump and is bent over a bridge, examining a red signal. The small light turns green. The train whistles and arrives. Already

Murad is talking to Sadiq, pointing at the engine. The two boys jump up and run towards the next bridge to catch another glimpse of the trains. Well, the talk about behaviour will have to wait for now.

Sadiq squeaks delightedly and Murad emits his strange cough-laugh as two trains simultaneously pull away in opposite directions. Murad bounces upright, followed by Sadiq and they hop across the stone bridge. Arjun watches his son move swiftly through the narrow path of a typical country village, ignoring the beautiful Tudor-detailed houses, the church spire, the groomed field with its polo players. The boys cross another bridge and vanish among the shrubs as they drop to watch some other train. Murad has his absorbed look, the one he has when he sinks into a book, his left hand resting on the chair arm, right forefinger and thumb rubbing the top corner of the next page, the story sinking him deeper. Arjun breathes in as he watches Sadiq who, from the back, might be a younger version of Murad. The oddest impression of Murad leading his younger self through this tiny world.

A flick of colour announces Sadiq's hat as he follows Murad past a village pond. They are talking intently about something. Strange. Murad, so inadequately dressed, looks more comfortable here than Arjun in his warm clothes and sensible shoes. Suddenly it comes to him: Murad doesn't care what these people think of him. He cares about his studies, his music, his friends, the operation of these small trains. It's probably Murad's British education. Arjun is proud of his intellectual son, and a little wistful. It would be nice to feel you could just walk into any place like this one and enjoy the sights. Go here, go there, without thinking that others are watching and judging whether you were being too Indian.

A young Indian girl in a blue and green shalwar khameez under a black jacket catches his eye. How sweetly she takes care of her younger sister. They pass over the bridge and the little one tugs her to stop to admire the boats. Arjun sees she's wearing *chappals* over thin socks. Sandals in this weather? She must be Murad's age. She looks a little like Pavitra when she was young: the slim figure, the long tapered fingers, the gentle expression.

With a start, he realizes he hasn't seen Pavi in over a week. They didn't have their usual lunch last weekend since she was busy with her welfare work, bundling up bales of clothes to send to Africa. He'd dropped Sunila over to help and had a cup of tea while the women worked. They argued about some blue coat of Pavi's that Pavi thought the Africans could use. It was a nice wool one, quite new-looking too. Surely an African wouldn't need something so heavy? Sunila had been tight-lipped about it. But, after all, it was Pavi's coat to give away. So generous. She gives away so much that he sometimes wonders if she is still trying to fill the hole left by Mum's passing. She took a long time to recover from that.

These days she's much quieter. He puts it down to having kids and adjusting to the responsibilities of married life.

Aren't they all quieter, slower, less likely to laugh? Pavi was always one for laughing. So lively, so full of unexpected ideas.

She turned up at his office once, back in Bombay, where he'd taken his first job as a junior accountant for Carstairs and Sons. He was scheduled to play in the Under 21 Squash Racquets Championship after work. He'd seen the notice: a recruiting coach would be visiting from the Maharashtra Squash Racquets Team. They had started to win tournaments against the British Squash Racquets Club. Certainly, the English won more often but, still, the idea that they could be beaten by the Maharashtrans...

He'd repeatedly hauled back his wriggling focus to the columns of figures in the large black ledgers. Surely he'd qualified in enough tournaments? He went over each win, added each point, re-estimated his current ranking. Maybe nineteen was too young to be considered for such a respected team. Maybe there were others who'd accumulated more points. Maybe he just wasn't good enough.

As he arrived at the Maharashtra Club, he found Pavi, her face like Christmas morning.

'What are you doing here?'

'I skipped out of school. Look, I've got something for you. Hurray for Team Arjun!' She held out a sumptuous green and gold Maharashtra Team jumper.

One hand lifted to touch the jumper. '*Arré*, Pavi. What if someone sees? Assuming, and all. I'm *junior* team, isn't it? I'm not even picked.' His language fell apart from its usual careful English and the last word came out as *pick-ud*.

'They *will* pick you, *bhai*. I'll keep this until after. Go and change, now. I'll be right in the front, shouting my lungs out.' And Pavitra tucked the jumper back into her bag and marched off to the outside stands reserved for the non-British. She was right. He'd won his match and a place on the Maharashtra Team, and he'd worn his new jumper home.

So long ago. Arjun shrugs the past away and moves on to the next village. Perhaps he should have invited Pavitra along to Bekonscot. She'd have admired everything, *s-o-o sweet, so clever*, and thoroughly enjoyed a mug of tea at the café. But this is meant to be a bonding experience for himself and Murad, who is…

On the other side of the lake, Murad is standing next to the signal box. Sadiq and two other small boys are peering through the window. The signalman comes out and beckons. The three youngsters bundle in, but Murad hesitates. The man beckons again and, hands stuffed in pockets, Murad slips in. The door closes. Arjun imagines the operations board, the lights, the levers, Murad taking it all in, silent at first. Before long, he'll be asking about the gauge radii, the trains' chassis, diesel versus steam engines, the classic 'Blue Peter' train and the construction of the Manor House Tunnel.

Arjun stops at a village where ships are unloading their catch. It does look like one of the south-east coastal towns,

like Ramsgate or Wells-next-the-Sea. The shops with
green and white awnings, the small boats tied up by the
dock, a few hikers precariously near the cliff edge, while
the most convincing detail is the grey, cold weather. He
realizes he knows England: these small towns with their
dripping ice cream and nasty pink rock that the kids so
love, the A40 and its roundabouts, the Underground, St
James's Park, the endless dark of winter only matched by
the British capacity for complaining about it. He's been
here for fifteen years. It's a shock to realize how the time
has passed by. So, he is British in some way. How Jonti
would laugh at him. *Still Indian but British also, isn't it?*

For a moment he wonders if Haseena and Nawal are
enjoying their film. He is practising thinking about them
together, his sisters-in-law, so that he doesn't have to think
about Haseena under the trees in Richmond Park, when
he moved in too close. The shock in her face when she
realized he was trying to kiss her. It was a mistake. She
looked so lovely, sitting on the grass for their picnic, her
cream and silver sari spread around her. Sadiq had been
off climbing some fallen tree. If she hadn't shifted over to
pass the chicken, if he hadn't dithered over the drumstick
or the breast, if she hadn't smiled and offered him a paper
plate. He'd made a fool of himself. He breathes out quickly.
How could he have done something like that in public?
What if someone had seen?

At least she never told Sunila. Sometimes he wonders if
Sunila knows. He shakes his head. Ridiculous to dwell on

such nonsense. Maybe a brisk walk around the miniature lake.

His feet are beginning to feel numb. Perhaps the boys would like a cup of tea, too. He slowly walks towards the signal box. He steps back off the narrow path to allow three excited small boys, a sullen teenage girl and two adults to pass. The adults take their time, not noticing Arjun. The woman finally notices him. 'Come on, Clifford. You're standing in front of someone.'

Clifford glances behind, scratches a large pink ear. 'Oops, sorry. No offence, mate.' His wife hauls him away.

Arjun doesn't move immediately. His right leg feels strange. *Not here. Not in the middle of Bekonscot Village.* He carefully transfers his weight to his left leg. He looks down. He is standing in the mud. There is nothing to lean on. Another large family comes rushing by. They don't see him, a small Indian man standing in the shrubbery. They pass around the corner and he hears a child's voice. 'It's a real army barracks, Mum.'

Now he is trapped, a foreign addition to the landscaping. He imagines himself suddenly dwindling to miniature. What would his role be at Bekonscot? They could place him just outside the perimeter of the army barracks. *Native prisoner caught escaping.* A semicircle of soldiers aiming rifles at him.

His shoes are dirtied. The thought of being covered in muck makes him shudder. He tries to move but his right leg won't budge. He is no longer a visitor entitled to stroll around, buy tea at the café or browse through the postcards. He is something else: a nuisance, a loiterer, visibly out of place. Any official seeing him might assume that he's up to no good. The thought of being seen as someone doing something even faintly unacceptable… He has struggled so hard to blend in and now he is a focal point. He shifts his weight, gingerly trying out his right leg. Please let the leg be all right. And, suddenly, it is. He is free to step back onto the path.

Murad and Sadiq round the corner and stop in front of him.

'Oh. There you are. I was just coming to find you.' Arjun tries to speak normally over the dissipating embarrassment.

'Uncle, *look* at your shoes! *You* won't get any chocolate biscuits for tea.' Sadiq's round eyes. Murad's snort.

'Someone stood in front of me. Huge fellow. I had to step off the path to avoid being trampled on.' It is meant to be funny: Arjun as a bewildered Buster Keaton figure, the others as the bumbling Keystone Cops. Jonti would have known how to make it into a joke. Arjun clears his throat.

'So, Sadiq. Did you like the signal box? Did you run any of the trains?'

'Only the *signalman* can perform operations,' Murad says.

'But we saw *everything*, didn't we, Murad? And the man—'

'—the *signalman*—'

'Yes, him. He said we could come and *work* there.' Sadiq beams. 'I'm going to pass all my exams and then I can

build a new track through a mountain. I'm going to make
the mountain as well.'

Arjun buys cream cakes for the boys. Sadiq has lemonade
and Murad has tea. Murad takes huge bites of the cake,
chewing and swallowing as though the cake is something
shameful to be dealt with as efficiently as possible. Sadiq
pokes out fingerfuls of cream as he continues to outline his
plan for a mountain, a forest and a family of three-toed
sloths that he's been reading about. Arjun sips his tea,
grateful for the warmth of the thick china mug. How to
get Murad, his son with fifteen O-levels, to talk?

'Ah, how are your studies going?'

Murad, finishing his cake, makes a strange gulping
noise.

Arjun tries again. 'Do you like any of your classes?'

Shrug.

A pattern of cracks in the white mug's glazing leads
the eye through a maze to blank whiteness. 'Do they have
woodwork?'

'Yeah.'

'I'm doing woodwork next year, Uncle. I'm going to
make Mum a cheeseboard.'

'Very nice, Sadiq.' Arjun tries to keep Murad talking.
'Maths?' He keeps his voice strictly neutral as he turns
the mug. Another maze appears on the mug and just as
abruptly stops.

'I love maths. Do you love maths, Murad?' Sadiq swings
his legs and sucks at the lemonade.

The next pause is a long one. Finally, Murad relents. 'Maths. Chemistry. And biology. Biochemistry.'

What on earth is biochemistry? It sounds dangerous.

Murad studies his empty plate. 'It's the study of chemical processes in living organisms. It's new. Our chemistry teacher, Mr Randall, told us about it. He's one of the pioneers.' Something softens in Murad's face. 'Two separate sciences, but they're connected.' He softly repeats the word. 'Connected.' An old Murad-habit of iteration, to hear again how the words sound.

'Can you blow things up? I can't *wait* to do chemistry. It's called "stinks".'

'Sadiq. You should call it "chemistry".' Arjun tries for propriety.

'And biology is called "bilge".' Sadiq yawns. 'Can I go to the toilet?'

Arjun takes Sadiq to the gents, offers to stay with him and is loftily waved away.

Back at the table, he decides to risk a question. 'Is this biochemistry offered at any university?'

'Mr Randall says Cambridge.' Murad says this in a way that indicates he understands Cambridge is some impossibly distant country where he will not go. 'But there are others. Cardiff, Sussex, Leicester.'

'Three A-levels. That's the usual load, isn't it?'

'I'll have to take S-levels as well. It's competitive.' Murad's voice is soft, as though he doesn't want anyone to hear him talking about competing.

The two years of brain-grinding drudgery required to take A-levels are bad enough. How will Murad handle scholarship exams?

He clears his throat. 'You want to take S-levels?'

'Three A-levels and two S-levels.'

Arjun coughs, sips his tea. 'Murad, I have always said that you are a highly intelligent boy.'

He ignores the lifting shoulder as Murad body-blocks the words.

'I believe you can do this A-levels and S-levels.' Arjun feels his language cracking apart under the strain. 'Very hard work, but you can do it, isn't it?' He sounds like Sunila. He clears his throat. 'What I am saying is that we are behind you all the way.'

'Mr Randall runs a study group. After school. He's coaching the S-level boys.' Murad is breathless with imparting so much personal information. 'He says he wants me to take S-level biology and chemistry. He says I can pass.'

Arjun suppresses a smile of sheer pleasure at his son's pride, at the acknowledgement of the teacher and the boy's excitement over whatever this biochemistry may be.

'Of course.' Arjun empties his cup. 'Of course you should take them. And of course you will pass.'

'Hullo.' Sadiq is back. 'Can we have another cake, Uncle?'

Arjun's son. Going to university. 'Go and choose the one you want.' He lifts his chin at Murad. 'You too, son.' He hands over a pound note.

'Thanks, Dad.' Murad half-smiles.

Arjun feels his chest grow with pride. A-levels and S-levels. Murad will be eighteen by the time he takes these exams. It's all happening so quickly. He can report to Sunila that her silent son is going to an English university.

He glances at his watch. There will be enough time to have fish and chips on the way to Haseena's house. The boys come back and Murad gives Arjun the change. Murad tells Sadiq a joke and Sadiq hiccups with laughter. Arjun sits back, undoes the top button on his coat. It's suddenly warmer.

They head back through the village, the boys wandering ahead. Arjun wonders if Murad sees a carthorse pulling a plough, a cricket game, a windmill with sails gently turning, Argue & Twist Solicitors, Ivan Huven – Baker, a young boy in a red shirt running away from a bull with a lowered head.

They stop over the last narrow bridge as a steam train puffs underneath. Murad crouches as the train stops at the station. Arjun admires the way he straightens up in one effortless move, laughs at something Sadiq says and walks on towards the exit.

The small train puffs more steam, emits a squeaky toot and trundles unevenly away across a field where four plastic ducks bob unconvincingly on a pond with a life-size leaf floating near the edge. Arjun waits while the last carriage finally disappears into a tunnel and turns to follow his son.

5

INHERITING THE GENE FLAW

JANUARY 1970

'Put on something warmer. And not black. You're too young to wear black. Pick a nice colour. Pink or something.' Arjun watches his daughter stamp upstairs to change out of her black corduroys and black sweater. Tarani was never an easy child, but that's nothing compared to how she is at thirteen. She hates the phrase 'earliteen'. She hates anything he says to her.

He calls up the stairs. 'And don't be long. We're leaving in five minutes.'

Sunila and Murad have gone to Pavi's and he is to take Tarani with him to visit Haseena. The children have been fighting again. Murad, sixteen, mocks Tarani's skinny, childish frame and the desperate way she counts the few hairs in her armpits. He wants to tell Murad, *Let her be*. But Murad has a new, fierce armour that repels everything that doesn't immediately concern him. Obviously, good manners are no longer necessary.

These days, Murad only has time for his bodybuilding. Arjun has heard the painful squeaking of springs behind Murad's door and once saw the chest expander protruding from under the bed. Murad is making himself into a different person, one who will never have sand kicked in his face providing he actually makes it to a beach.

Sunila tells Tarani to ignore Murad's teasing, but she can't. Her face crumples each time her brother jeers at her. Arjun feels the word-hooks, feels the bleeding below the skin, tries to think of something to say that will heal her. But she has no time for him either. He is also the enemy. She narrows her shoulders against him, squeezes herself inwards so that no one can reach her. She is gradually turning concave. He wants to tell her to stand upright, to push her shoulders back. He has tried to get her to play squash. It would boost her confidence. But she refuses, says it's too hard.

Tarani comes clumping downstairs disguised as a chameleon: green skirt with an Indian design of elephants and a neon-pink t-shirt under a dull-orange hand-knitted sweater that Sunila gave her two Christmases ago, never worn until now. She lifts her chin, waiting for his disapproval, waiting for him to send her upstairs to change again. But Arjun doesn't want to see what alternatives she can find.

He clears his throat. 'That's a nice skirt. Did Pavitra Aunty give you?'

'Haseena Aunty.' The voice is packed with cold anger. And there's something else, too: the agony of being small and unattractive. His heart contracts for her. She will walk out of the house looking like a carnival clown purely to *show* him. Her black stockings sag around the knees and ankles. Her shoes, school lace-ups, are unpolished.

'Come. Sit down.' His voice is gentle, and he sees her glance at him. He motions to the stairs and she sits, waiting for him to say something. He rummages under the stairs for the bag of shoe polish that only he uses.

He lays out the black Kiwi wax, brush and soft cloth and, beginning with the left shoe, uses a brush to apply the polish. He balances her foot on his bent knee as he brushes and buffs the leather until it gleams dully. Tarani, thin hands grasped together, looks down at her newly polished shoe.

'See what a little effort can do?' He polishes her other shoe, ties her shoelaces, collects the brush, polish and cloth and puts the bag away. 'If you do this your shoes will always look nice.'

She is still sitting on the stairs staring up at him, as though he's just told her a secret. Her eyes are large and slightly scared. 'Thanks, Dad.'

'All right. Let's go.' Underneath all the sulky resentment and rude behaviour is *fear*? Why? He's always loved her so dearly. What has made her afraid?

She pulls on the heavy, hairy camel-coloured coat that makes her look, as Murad says, like a yeti. At least she will be warm. He wraps his wool scarf around his neck and pulls on his thick parka and lined leather gloves.

The morning is flint-edged, sun sparkling off the frost on the pavement, hedges and trees. Clouds of their warm breath pulse ahead as they walk to catch the bus. Tarani glances down at her shoes. Sometimes, she kicks one foot out a little further, just to see the polished leather, pretending that she's kicking the last of the dead black leaves iced onto the pavement. He can't remember when he did anything that made her so happy. Halfway across the field they spot the bus coming along the Uxbridge Road and race to the bus stop. Tarani giggles as she runs. By the time they climb aboard, he is laughing, too.

He pays their bus fare and she looks at him.

'Well, you're getting fast.' He hands her a bus ticket.

'I'm not that fast.'

'I used to run faster than you.'

'You still can, Dad.' She rolls the ticket into a tight cylinder.

'I'm serious. You could run really well if you wanted to. You have the right frame, and you can accelerate quickly.' Accelerate. He makes her sound like a car.

'There's loads of kids in my class who are faster than me.'

'There *are* loads of kids. It's a plural.' The correction is automatic. 'Anyway, I could teach you how to run.'

'I wouldn't be any good.' Already she's turning away from the subject.

'What's your time for the hundred?'

She shrugs. 'I don't know.'

One moment she is close, a small child again, reaching for his hand. The next she is gone, her narrow shoulders closing around her. *I don't want you.* It is easy to slide from this one moment to recollections of others: the refusal of eye contact, the bare skimming of his cheek with her reluctant kiss, the deliberately ugly clothes, her nail-biting even though he has taken time to show her how to trim and shape her nails.

'Sit up straight. You're ruining your posture.'

She jerks herself upright and stares out of the window. He glances at her profile: the thin long nose with its tiny bump. He calls her Big Nose but secretly loves the shape of it. It isn't one of those forgettable noses. Hers is distinctive, meant for great things. She could be a leader, perhaps even like Indira Gandhi, although Mrs Gandhi is quite ugly. And Tarani is going to be a beauty, despite the bitten fingernails and scrawny legs. She sometimes reminds him of Mughal paintings: long hands with fingertips that curve back, eyes that tilt up at the corners, high-arched eyebrows. He'd shown her the pictures but she turned away, repelled by anything Indian. She insisted, 'I'm *English.*' And his response, 'You're Indian. I'm an Indian father and you are my daughter.' He wanted to show his love, but she stamped upstairs, face frozen in anger.

He glances at her again, her face turned away. She thinks she is inscrutable with her careful blank expressions, forgetting that every little transitional flash of feeling is telegraphed as surely as if she has shouted at the top of her lungs. Poor Tarani, trying so hard to be like Murad. Murad has never had much in the way of facial expressions, so his metamorphosis to unsmiling Sphinx is more credible. Murad, with his belief that his spring contraption will make him popular with the girls; it's enough to make you weep if it weren't so funny. If only there were some way to tell Murad that to have girls like you, you just have to be yourself. Surely it's not so hard to understand. But who is Murad when he is himself? The morose eye-contact-avoiding boy who sits at the dining table? The strangely talkative cousin who entertains Sadiq? Is there yet another Murad whom Arjun doesn't know?

The rising volume of an exchange between the bus conductor and a tall, thin West Indian woman claims everyone's attention. The woman refuses to pay the bus fare for her three children who are all, she claims, under twelve. Two of them are old enough to stare back coldly at the curious faces. The passengers hang intently on the argument, some of them shaking their heads in delighted disapproval. *Who does she think she is?* The oldest, a boy with a strip of dark fuzz on his upper lip, mutters a curse at the conductor and there's a collective gasp of horror. His mother extends one arm and clips him around the head, dislodging his red-yellow-and-green-striped knitted hat. He makes the mistake of pursing his lips and making some indecent sucking noise. His mother uses her free arm and then her handbag to belabour him, screaming high-pitched abuse. In one athletic movement, he snatches up his hat and is halfway up the stairs when the conductor furiously rings the bell, shouting, 'Off! *Now*. All of you.'

The bus halts, the driver craning over his shoulder as the family tumbles off. Arjun sees the boy scanning the bus. He stands there, sneering, in his red-and-black bell-bottom jeans and orange flowered shirt, the halo of frizzy hair sticking up everywhere. Probably doesn't brush his teeth either. The mother slams her hand into the side of the bus as it drives off. The passengers tut to each other. Arjun is relieved; at least she isn't Indian. The other people on the bus must see that *he* isn't from the West Indies. He is sitting quietly, fare paid, with his quiet daughter who now turns to him with a wide smile.

'Did you *see* them?'

Arjun clears his throat. 'When you are in public places, you must behave appropriately.'

'They were *funny*.'

'They were not funny.' His voice is low. 'They were rude and the bus conductor was right to throw them off.'

Tarani's voice is too loud. 'But the bus conductor was rude to *them*. He kept saying they had to pay full fare.'

'Two of the children were obviously teenagers.'

'How do you *know*? What if they weren't?'

He laughs his false laugh, the one he uses when he doesn't have an answer. How can he explain the muscular build of the two boys, their cocky adolescent behaviour? He hesitates: but what if she's right? He glances around,

pretending to look up at the advertisements next to the
bell cord. There is a smell of righteousness in the air. Here
and there people speak up: 'You were right, Freddie. You
don't want to stand for that nonsense.' Freddie busies
himself with collecting fares.

Arjun, too, would like to say something, but what if he
is seen as *one of them*? Some people don't see the difference
between West Indians and Indians. How ignorant the
British are, as Jonti would say.

Tarani has turned back to the window. 'The conductor
was *wrong*.'

'He was doing his job. Those people were—'

She whips around to face him. 'There are boys like
that at school. They're younger than me but they just
look older.'

He is stunned. There are black children at her school?
He swallows. He must be calm. After all, this is a progressive
society. Everyone mixes with everyone else.

'So, you know these boys at your school?'

'Don't be—' She catches herself. 'I'm not *friends* with
them. They're *younger*.' She stares at the long cascade of
blonde hair of the girl sitting in front. 'They're always in
trouble. But Janice, she's West Indian. She says everyone
expects them to get in trouble. So.' She turns away as though
everything is now clear.

Tarani has a black friend? He clears his throat again.
'So, your friend, Janice?'

'It's our stop.' She stands up and pulls the cord.

By the time they're off the bus and walking through the side streets to Haseena's house, the idea of Janice has almost vanished with their cold breath, but still he tries to catch up with it. Perhaps Janice is a good student, despite her background.

'Have you and Janice been friends long?'

'She's not my friend.'

Beat.

'Well, she *is* my friend. But she's not with my *other* friends. We talk sometimes. I like her. She makes me laugh.'

So, a boisterous West Indian girl. Just as he thought. He is anxious. What if this girl introduces Tarani to reggae? He has heard terrible things about reggae and how it makes children want to take drugs. He wants to ask Tarani about drugs. Has she been offered any? Has she seen anyone taking them? He has no idea what they might look like. His medical training has taught him nothing about street drugs.

They arrive at Haseena's house and ring the bell. Haseena, fresh and beautiful in a simple blue and white sari, embraces Tarani. 'You are lovelier each time I see you. Isn't she, Arjun?'

He tilts his head, not yes, not no. He cannot help this tightening of the stomach each time he sees her. They don't embrace; she briefly touches his shoulder.

'You're a real beauty.' Haseena takes both of Tarani's hands. 'Come, I have some things for you to look at.' She glances at Arjun. 'Tea is ready to pour in the kitchen.

And chocolate biscuits. Help yourself. We won't be long. Girl-talk.'

Arjun follows a familiar scent into the kitchen. He stands at the doorway admiring the range of neatly hung pots over the stove. How orderly everything is: plates displayed on shelves, mugs hung on a wooden stand. On the table a cardboard box is piled with what looks like underwear. Arjun is momentarily surprised, but the box turns out to hold small, plump, oval- and heart-shaped cushions, delicately sewn in cream and rose-pink satin, with lace trim and pale gold and grey velvet ribbon. How long it must have taken to sew all of these. He examines one. The stitches are almost invisible. It sits neatly in the hand, cool and satisfying to hold. He likes to think of these little cushions going to good homes. The old ladies will love them, pressing their noses against the soft material and thinking of long-ago summers on lawns when not-yet-gone-to-college boys played cricket.

Over two years since Richmond Park. They've handled it well, he and Haseena. He's been careful about not phoning, not visiting. She's never mentioned that one unfortunate event. But then it's not as though she has anything to complain about anyway. He never actually did anything. Attractive women dress to attract men. That's all there is to it. They can't blame men for paying attention.

But somehow trotting out the old argument isn't as convincing as it used to be. He slips the sachet back into the box.

He pours tea into one of Haseena's plain white teacups, props two chocolate biscuits on the edge of the saucer and sits at the kitchen table. He sips his tea and looks over the flat-cropped parallel hedges of lavender bushes streaming down to the end of the garden path. Sunila would like this. Perhaps he can suggest they grow lavender. He imagines them choosing the plants, putting them in the soil together, nurturing the seedlings, discussing soil acidity. In reality, she will want to plant in the sun and he will want to plant in the shade. She will knead in handfuls of plant food, too much for the delicate seedlings. He will want to prune to encourage growth. She will want to snip off stalks for her flower arrangements. Why can't they see things the same way once in a while?

A high laugh. Tarani. Murmuring of voices and footsteps on the stairs. He sits a little straighter. He wants to compliment Haseena on her hard work and artistry. But as they enter he can only look at Tarani. She is wearing a white, baggy blouse tucked into bell-bottomed blue jeans and shiny red shoes with thick crêpe platforms. She looks at least five inches taller.

'Isn't she trendy?' Haseena twirls a laughing Tarani around. 'She should be on the cover of a magazine!'

Tarani faces Arjun, a little shy but smiling, waiting for his compliment about how she looks in these ridiculous clothes. Arjun doesn't want to insult Haseena, who has clearly spent a lot, but he can't allow Tarani to go about looking like a clown. The bell-bottoms are so wide they'll trip her up when she walks. The puffy-sleeved blouse hangs on her thin frame instead of fitting her properly. And the ugly, clumping shoes. Surely she can't expect to walk in those?

'He's speechless.' Haseena looks at him. 'Come, let me pour some tea, Tarani. How many sugars do you want?'

But Tarani wants a response. 'Do you think I look trendy?' She tries out the word on him.

'I'm afraid I don't really know what trendy is.' He tries to be light-hearted, in the spirit of the occasion. 'The, uh, the blouse is quite nice.'

Haseena puts Tarani's tea on the table. 'Come, darling, and have your tea.' She turns back to Arjun. 'This is the height of fashion. It's the *look*.' Haseena brings over the plate of McVitie's. 'It's flowing, casual. Free. She looks gorgeous.'

'Free.' Tarani throws her arms out and pivots. She staggers in the platform shoes. 'Oops!'

'Come sit down, darling, before you twist your ankle.' Haseena laughs.

'Or break your neck,' Arjun offers. 'Those things are dangerous.'

'I love them, Aunty!' Tarani is still heady with being beautiful. 'I'm getting used to them already.'

'Haseena, you took so much trouble.' Arjun examines the trousers that balloon around Tarani's legs.

'No trouble.' Haseena smiles. 'And the shoes are from a friend. They don't fit her daughter, so she gave them to me.'

'They're groovy. Thank you so much, Aunty.' Tarani hugs her aunt and sits down.

'Your mother won't approve.' Arjun tries to make it into a joke but Tarani's face empties.

'Have a biscuit.' Haseena pushes the plate towards Tarani.

Arjun clears his throat. Doesn't Tarani realize people will laugh at her? 'You've been busy.' He picks out one of Haseena's lavender sachets from the box. 'Very nice.' He smooths out the lace. 'Tasteful. Delicate colours. Something that people will love to buy. Something they can be proud of having.'

Silence.

Beside him, Tarani makes a sudden movement, knocks the table. Tea slip-slops into the saucers.

The front door is thrown open and they hear high, clear singing. 'Oh, food, fabulous, food, beautiful, food, glo-ri-ous food!'

Ten-year-old Sadiq, hair sticking up, shirt hanging out, sweater struggling over one shoulder, trousers streaked with mud, enters and flings his arms wide. 'Thank you, thank you. You're a beautiful audience. I'm *starving*. Oh. Hullo Uncle. Hullo Tarani.' He offers himself to Arjun for a dutiful hug.

Sadiq, so much like Jonti. Arjun smiles. 'So? How are you, Sadiq? Doing well at school?'

'Yes-thank-you-Uncle.' Sadiq throws himself around his mother's neck and suddenly straightens up. 'Tarani, you look like a real dolly bird!'

Tarani is startled. 'Pardon?'

'You should be on telly. Shouldn't she, Mum?' He turns back to Tarani. '*Top of the Pops.*'

'Me?' Arjun can see that Tarani is ready for Sadiq to say *Just kidding!*

'I mean, some girls are too fat to wear bell-bottoms, but you look all right.'

'Thanks.' Tarani pushes her hair back.

Haseena unwinds Sadiq's arms from her neck. 'Yes, my noisy rambunctious son, she does look stunning.' Haseena smooths Sadiq's startled-looking hair. 'What have you got in your hair? Car oil?'

Sadiq ducks away and grabs a biscuit. 'Oh, hey.' He picks up one of the sachets. 'Mum *made* all of these. We're going to have a shop. Did she tell you?'

'It's a small flower shop in Hounslow. We've talked on the phone and they're willing to share their space. We're meeting them next week,' Haseena explains as she hands cutlery to Tarani and Sadiq, who go into the dining room to set the table.

He can hear the giggling.

'Congratulations, Haseena. You and Nawal deserve this.' Arjun is pleased for her.

'Thank you, *bhai.*'

He watches her deft movements as she transfers the curry and rice from pans to serving dishes. He's watched Sunila do exactly the same things at home, so how is it that Haseena looks so different? Suddenly, like opening a small box crammed with old Christmas decorations, their showy glitter faded and irrelevant, the pushed-down feelings come surging up.

'Haseena, I've never said anything to you.'

She is busy ladling dhal into a bowl. 'About what?'

'Richmond Park. I wanted to – I'm so sorry—' His heart is almost throttling him.

'Please, *bhai*.' Haseena places the ladle carefully on a small plate and turns around. 'Let's not talk about it.'

'But I've never apologized to you. All this time.'

She steps forward and for one moment he thinks she will take his hand. 'It was just a mistake. I don't even think about it.'

'But I—'

She holds one hand out, palm flat against an invisible wall. 'It's past and forgotten.' She smiles, turns the palm up. 'We're still friends, yes?'

He nods. 'Yes, of course.'

Friends? This is all?

She picks up the ladle. Straightens the pot of dhal. 'Any news, *bhai*? From the hospital?'

He clears his throat. 'Just tests. You know how they take their time. But I'm fine. I played squash this week. Thrashed some young kid who thought he knew what he was doing.' He doesn't mention that his leg wouldn't allow him out of bed this morning. He had to wait another five minutes before it would agree to move.

Tarani comes back in to ask what else she can do. She takes bowls of food to the table, fills water glasses, folds napkins. You'd think she was enjoying herself. Why can't she be like this at home?

Sadiq is attempting to juggle with two of the sachets. 'You can buy one if you like. They're only five pounds.'

'What nonsense, Sadiq.' Haseena catches the sachets mid-flight and returns them to the box. 'They're one pound each. And they're for the sale at the church.'

'Oh, please, Mum. Just one more try. I can juggle under my leg, look. If I just stand like this—' He falls.

Tarani is laughing. Arjun, despite himself, is smiling. Their smiles flick across each other, hesitate, almost withdraw, and then the complicit our-family-is-so-bizarre understanding. He feels his chest flooded with relief. She still likes him. He picks up his tea and sips, watches Tarani's shoulders relax and her body curve into a chair as she talks with Sadiq, laughs at his descriptions of singing exercises.

Of course Tarani will have to change into her normal clothes for the journey home, but let her keep these things. Maybe she can wear them at weekends around the house. He feels himself expand. It is good to allow these little indulgences. He wishes he might reach out his hand and smooth her hair, just a single touch. He sets his teacup carefully in the saucer.

6

A NORMAL LIFESPAN

FEBRUARY 1971

Hampton Court. In the bitter cold, when anyone with a grain of sense would be at home, not tramping around some draughty old mansion. 'Palace,' Arjun says. 'A good idea to come when it's not overrun with tourists,' he says. 'And it's free.' As always, Arjun sticks to his idea like a dog to a tree. If he decides to take the children out, that's it; and Sunila must be dragged along, too. *The family should be together.* It doesn't matter that she is with the children all week; their grumbling and complaining and forgetting their lunch money, their dirty clothes (how can two children be so filthy?), their endless quarrelling that she hides from Arjun so that he won't discipline them. By the weekend she is tired of them.

She glances behind at Murad and Tarani sitting in separate seats. Murad stares straight ahead, arms crossed.

Tarani looks out of the train's window, down at her hands, fiddles with her hair, anything to avoid looking at her father sitting in front of her.

How the young can hate. It happens so quickly, so easily for them. One moment they are in the kitchen, laughing over some joke, and then Tarani is silent in her room, hair over her face, wounded over some imagined insult, some conversation that went wrong, some wild idea she's had that Arjun has mockingly dismissed. They are so alike, she and Arjun: the same quick manner of expressing themselves, the same sense of humour, sudden anger, sudden generosity. They even use their hands the same way when they speak. When they argue it's like watching two mad, rival conductors swiping and slashing the air between them.

Arjun keeps his feelings to himself about these conflicts. His position, as usual, is inflexible. *I am an Indian father and she is my daughter.* Tarani, however much she wishes to contain the hurt, cannot. Sunila hears the late-night muttered monologues as Tarani treads and retreads conversations, clumping around in those foolish platform shoes that Haseena gave her. Sometimes, Sunila has sat on the stairs, listening to her daughter being witty, energetic, disdainful. It's almost as good as a play. Often Sunila can't make out the actual words, but Tarani's tone is exactly Arjun's: slightly boisterous, bullying, superior. She can even do his weary *all right then have it your own way* voice that shows he's right and everyone else is too stupid to understand. How has Tarani managed to reproduce Arjun's voice so accurately?

Sunila has longed to tap on the door, say 'I understand', but Tarani would be furious. Perhaps if Sunila had the courage to agree with Tarani, *yes, he is unfair,* her daughter might talk to her more. But Sunila has given her word: for better or worse. It isn't Christian to take sides against one's husband. And yet her heart goes out to Tarani. *I know what you're going through.* She prays about it. *Lord, please let them get along.* She sits with her Bible, the mainstay for most of her decisions. But Jesus wasn't married; He didn't have children. What use is Jesus in a situation like this? Of course, Jesus would have had some excellent advice if only someone had thought to ask about it and then write it down. What opportunities the disciples missed. And that Paul, so busy with his letters here, there and everywhere, couldn't he have slipped in a few questions to the Lord? Jesus was so gentle with the children, suffering them to come to Him. But how much would He have suffered teenagers with their snarky comments and their way of looking through you?

As they exit Hampton Court Station, Arjun doesn't respond to Sunila's comment about the nice clear day. The pale sun backs against the pale sky but there are none of the characteristically heavy winter clouds that hold snow or sleet. It is a cheering thought, this idea of a little sunshine in the middle of such an English winter. Let Arjun sulk in his winter coat. Today, Sunila will look for something bright; some colour, some winter flower that she can tuck away to remember as she goes through the week. And she can tell the girls at the office that she went to Hampton Court. *Such beautiful grounds. And they do a lovely tea, don't they?*

The pathway to the palace is frost-crisped as though it's been toasted in some Arctic oven. The Union Jack hangs limp between the sceptre-shaped chimneys. Let's see Bert chim-chiminey his way across that roof. Despite the arched entrance and the white gargoyles, there is something un-royal about the ordinary-looking brick. Grey scaffolding hedges some of the apartments.

They enter the Cartoon Gallery; the relief of being out of the cold. She examines the large paintings that don't look anything like cartoons. Many kings and queens must have walked through this gallery. Sunila doesn't know who they are but surely something of them is still here. She can imagine it: the sigh of a brocade dress along the wooden floor, the tap of a red-heeled shoe, the genteel conversation. What did they talk about, those old royals? Cleaning the chimneys? The plans for the next ball? Whose head to chop off?

'Come on, Mum, we're going to the maze.' Murad comes up and takes her arm. She is grateful for his firm support – *what a handsome boy he is* – even though she has no need of it.

'Look at these lovely hedges. So many interesting shapes. Look, there's a bear.'

'Topiary,' Murad says.

'So much more attractive than the normal bushes, although I'm sure they look nice, too.' God did, after all, make the bushes. What would He think of his creations being shaped into birds and animals?

'Murad, is Tarani all right?'

Murad grunts.

'Does that mean yes or no?'

'Don't know.'

'She hasn't said anything to you?'

Murad hesitates. 'What about?'

'Nothing. Just, you know. She seems quiet.' Sunila is hungry for what her fourteen-year-old daughter is up to and Murad probably knows.

Murad doesn't answer. He's taking his A- and S-level mocks this year. No wonder he's preoccupied.

Arjun turns to call to them, 'Let's all go in together.'

But Tarani has already disappeared into the maze.

Arjun is irritated. 'She'll get lost. I'm not going to search about for her.'

Murad slips past Sunila and Arjun into the maze.

'Murad. Wait for us.' But Murad has gone. Arjun turns to Sunila. 'You can't ask them to do one simple thing. Haven't I spoken about how dangerous it is to go running into the maze willy-nilly?'

Sunila bites the inside of her cheek at the idea of running about in a maze willy-nilly.

But Arjun has caught her expression. 'Go ahead and laugh. We'll see who'll be crying soon.'

They stand hesitantly at the maze's entrance. 'Well, we may as well go in.' Arjun walks ahead and Sunila follows.

How neatly they keep the hedges in here, too. Sunila admires the tall, square-cut shapes that rise perpendicularly all around. If it weren't a maze it would be quite disturbing. Just imagine being stuck in here. Is Tarani all right?

Sunila bumps into Arjun, who is coming back. 'Dead end. Let's try a different path.'

She stands aside to let him choose the next turning. They follow that one successfully for a while until a right turn takes them to another dead end.

She remembers something. 'Jonti came here, didn't he? Haseena found the middle straight away.'

Jonti had thrown his hands in the air. 'Nawal and I were both going hither and thither. Where is centre? Have you found centre? Shall we call for help? Nawal said, "What kind of outing is this? I can get lost by myself in Hounslow. I don't need any Hampton Court nonsense." And then these people with rucksacks came along. I said, "Nawal, darling, come. These people will know the way. Hikers and all." And when we finally arrive, Haseena was standing there. "Where have you been? I've been waiting for you." Cool as a cucumber. "Shall I lead you back now?" I was mad. Nawal was laughing and laughing. And they made me buy cream cakes. Such injustice, *bhai*. When did these women get so cheeky?'

'Haseena.' Arjun stops. 'Haseena told me…' He turns left and his voice is lost.

Sunila hurries around the corner. 'Told you what?'

' … a boyfriend.'

'Who has a boyfriend? Nawal?' Nawal would never look at anyone else. What nonsense, a boyfriend.

'Haseena…' Arjun's voice comes through the hedge separating them.

Sunila is irritated. 'Can you just stay in one place while I catch up?'

Arjun is waiting when Sunila turns the corner. 'Haseena has a boyfriend.'

The word is wrong. Kids have boyfriends and girlfriends. Haseena is forty. What does she want with a boyfriend? What on earth do they talk about? Their dead spouses?

'Who?' Sunila reaches for Arjun's arm, but he is already walking away around another corner.

His voice comes back faintly. 'Someone she met at the shop.'

'What shop?' Sunila has a distressing vision of Haseena chatting to men over the carrots in Tesco's.

'The one they're leasing. Nawal and Haseena. You remember. For the lavender.'

The shop in Hounslow is doing well. Orders pouring in, they say. They went to Paris for a week last September. How nice for them. Arjun has money. He could have taken her to Paris, too, but they ended up on day trips to Stonehenge and Cheddar Gorge.

'…I told her…' Arjun's voice disappears again and Sunila tries to work out which way his voice went. Was it further along the path or did he take this left-hand turn?

She looks up at the towering hedges. If only they had thought to cut little holes in the hedges, then people could see where they were going.

' …she's been seeing him for a month…' Arjun's voice floats to her.

'Who? The shop owner?'

Sunila walks quickly along one path and then waits for Arjun's voice. It comes from much closer. There's a small gap at the base of the hedges and she catches a glimpse of his shoes.

'A banker. International banking, she says.' His voice sounds strangely bitter, but perhaps it's just the leaves blurring the sound.

'Arjun, I'm here. Just on the other side. Can you wait for me?'

'Walk along and turn right.'

But she turns right at the wrong corner and is still separated from him by long, implacable green walls. 'What bank is he with?'

Suddenly Arjun appears. 'Don't shout like that. Do you want everyone to hear our private business?'

She whispers. 'I'm sorry, but—'

'I don't know what bank. I don't know who he is.'

'Is it safe?'

'She's an adult. She can do what she wants.'

She puts a hand out. 'Is he – is he – Indian?'

'I don't know anything about him. I have to talk to her. Perhaps I can meet him.'

What is happening to the family? In the old days, people married and that was it. If your husband died, you became a widow. You didn't go about with boyfriends.

In this corner of the maze they may as well be in a cave, exchanging secrets. Sunila speaks softly. 'Should you go alone? To see Haseena?'

He clears his throat. 'It might be better.'

He says nothing for a while. She wishes there was a way she could touch his arm, show him she was on his side.

There is no one to offer advice. These days, the great-aunts sit mumbling over knitting. Mum is gone, Jonti is gone and Mike, well, he is family but even though he's English, she can't imagine sitting down over a cup of tea to discuss Haseena with him.

'Then go.' Her whisper comes out almost as a gasp. She has always suspected Haseena of having feelings for Arjun. And probably vice versa. But if Haseena must have a *boyfriend* it should be the right kind.

'I don't want her to think I'm interfering.' Arjun is looking down.

'But you are her brother-in-law. And the head of the family. I'm sure she'll want to talk to you about it anyway.'

He begins to move away. 'Who is he, anyway, chasing after a widow like that? And what is Haseena thinking?'

He's angry at the man, but he's also angry at Haseena. What does he mean? Sunila can't call out to him in case she upsets him.

Despite the boyfriend nonsense, Sunila feels sorry for Haseena, who started her own business, handled her son alone and has taken care of her sister. And Arjun will talk to her as though she is just a stupid woman. Sunila knows that this is the way Arjun always talks, but she is used to it and Haseena isn't. Is there some way to warn her?

She tries to imagine what it's like to be Haseena, to bring up her children alone. Perhaps it wouldn't be so bad, apart from the kids always fighting. And kids certainly don't want conversation, at least not hers. When did it all change? They used to run to her when she came home from work. It was *Mummy this* and *Mummy that* and what they'd learned and what their friends said. Now she may as well not exist. The sympathy for Haseena fades.

Arjun has walked ahead and she is alone again. She turns another corner and Tarani is walking towards her. 'Hello Mum. Are you still looking for the centre?'

'I don't care about the centre. I'm tired of this maze.'

Tarani links her arm through Sunila's. A few quick turns and they are out. It's hard to believe that all this time they were so close to the exit. They wait for Murad and Arjun to appear. It's even colder than before.

'Shall we wait inside?' Tarani is shuffling from foot to foot. 'We can see them when they come out.'

They plod along the gravel path and push through the doors into the warmth of the palace.

Tarani says, 'I put my hands in the hedge. It wasn't warm but it felt nice.'

Sunila wants to say something too, but she can't tell
Tarani that her aunt has a boyfriend. She looks down.
They keep the floors so well polished.

Tarani traces over the frost on the inside of one of
the small windowpanes. 'Why do we have to come here
anyway? It's always Hampton Court or Kew Gardens.
And now we'll have to have one of those stupid cream
teas.'

Sunila wants to tell her daughter to be grateful, to look
around her at this beautiful building. The English took
their superior architecture to India and the other colonies.
They taught the natives how to make ceilings. Ceilings
protected you from rats and snakes and the hell of the
Indian summers.

'I thought you liked cream cakes,' Sunila says.

'I do, but that's not the point, is it? We have to do it
because it's *his* idea and it's what we always do when we
come to this place.'

'You like the cakes, so what difference does it make
whose idea it is?'

Tarani lifts a hand: the long fingers, the thin tendons,
the smooth skin, the way the wrist bends. It looks like a
flower stem. Sunila wants to say this aloud, but Tarani
drops her arm.

'Forget it. I knew you wouldn't understand. You always
take his side.'

Sunila wants to shake her. *Don't you see how much he has to
worry about? His job, the bills, arranging the future for you and your*

brother. And everyone in the family comes running to him with their problems or asking for a loan. Now your favourite aunt is running off with some banker, ruining the family name, and it's your father who has to talk sense into her. And despite all of that, he thinks of us and tries to do something nice.

'Here they are. Dad looks cross.' Tarani sounds satisfied.

Murad is keeping up with Arjun even though it looks as though Arjun wishes to stride ahead. They will have to sit over their cream tea, no one making eye contact, the conversation as dried out as the scones. But at the last moment, as they take the stone steps two at a time, Murad says something and Arjun laughs. And although the sun doesn't break through, suddenly there is more light around the glass doors where Sunila and Tarani wait.

7

PROGRESSIVE LOSS OF NEURONS IN THE SPINAL CORD

MARCH 1972

The tie is uneven and he persists until it lies smoothly between the crisp collar wings of his white shirt. The old wall mirror gives him back an undulating version of his anxious frown.

'I don't know why you bother. It's only the hospital.' Sunila rubs her nose with the flat of her hand.

More than his leg, he is worried about Murad, who is expecting to pass all his A-levels but is struggling with his S-level chemistry. After Cardiff University sent their offer, conditional on him passing chemistry, he spent an entire weekend in his bedroom refusing everything Sunila cooked, but accepting the McVitie's chocolate biscuits Tarani smuggled in.

He eventually emerged with a fluff of facial hair. Arjun's heart ached for him, but the boy needed some purpose. 'Pull yourself together. And shave, for goodness' sake. You look like one of those hippies.'

Arjun tilts his head and inspects his Harris tweed jacket, the small, neat pattern of his brown silk tie, his fine wool trousers and the shining shoes. Sunila has polished them, grumbling because he insists on Kiwi and not one of those modern sprays. She says it's all the same. He knows it's not. The polish must soak into the leather for at least two hours, preferably overnight, and only after that can you brush and shine the shoes properly. She says she dislikes the smell of shoe polish. He guesses that she thinks of the hundreds of street corners where the shoe-shine boys, bent heads, bent backs, feet braced, steadily polish away the endlessly creeping Bombay dust.

He tucks the white handkerchief into his top pocket. 'Where's Murad?'

'At his preparation lesson with Mr Turrington. They have a double lesson today. Tests next week only.'

'Good. I'll be back after lunch.'

'*After*? What will you eat?'

'I'll get a sandwich or something.'

'What nonsense, a sandwich. I can make something for you to take.' She is already halfway down the stairs. 'There's some of that curry left. You can have it with rice. I'll put it in a Tupperware and wrap a fork in a napkin and put it in a plastic bag.'

'You think I can walk into the hospital with a Tupperware box of curry?'

He tries to look casual; she's watching him come downstairs. The left leg has been failing more frequently.

He'd ignored the doctor's advice to seek a specialist until his leg gave out on him when he was shaking hands with Pastor Hargreve and his wife after church. There was no warning that the leg was weak, no staggering, no gradual numbness. His leg vanished beneath him and he fell, grabbing at Mrs Hargreve's bosom before rolling down the three white steps. Mrs Hargreve screamed while her husband calmly rebuked her. 'Don't be an idiot, Maisy.'

The pastor collected Arjun from the pavement.

'My leg. I'm so sorry. I hope I didn't—'

'Oh no. I just – I thought it was a mouse or something.' Mrs Hargreve daintily tugged her sunflower-patterned jacket around her wide shoulders.

'A mouse? Jumping on your tits?' The Hargreves' daughter snorted. 'You thought it was your lucky day.'

'Rebecca, that's quite enough.' Pastor Hargreve helped Arjun back into the church.

And then came all the questions, the concern. He was used to listening to problems, counselling patience, mediating disputes. He had to swallow the kindness, and the aftertaste remained in his throat.

Haseena phoned. 'Arjun, *bhai*? Pavitra said you fell at church last week. You need a neurologist.' She sounded quite stern. Was it the effect of the break-up with her boyfriend?

For almost seven months last year, Haseena ignored the outraged family and went about with some person named Hadley, a divorced English banker who was fond of gambling. *Off to see the ponies.* Arjun went to Haseena's for lunch and talked to her in a calm and reasonable manner. Haseena politely listened and then went to dinner with Hadley at Brown's Hotel. The aunts and great-aunts sucked their teeth, held prayer vigils and predicted terrible things. It couldn't have been worse if he'd been a Muslim. Finally, in November, Nawal let it slip that the relationship had ended. No one found out why but the great-aunts, relieved to be off their aching knees, went back to their word puzzles.

'Arjun, you know what Jonti would have said.' Haseena was clearly anxious if she was playing the Jonti card.

'All right, Haseena. I'll ask for a referral.' He knew exactly what Jonti would have said. *Idiot to ignore, isn't it?*

He saw the specialist in December and now, three months later, he is on his way to his follow-up appointment. He walks to the bus stop with his elegant black cane. It's more of an accessory since he only has to lean on it occasionally for those moments when the leg decides to leave and he has to wait for it to come back. He thinks of it as though it's wandered away, has paused somewhere, while his impatient body frets for its return.

How does a living part of the body become a stranger, behave so differently without the rest of the body's consent?

He never used to consult any part of himself when he stood or walked or picked up a squash racquet. *I'm not myself today*. If part of him vanishes, then part of the intrinsic who-he-is also vanishes. Who is left? He listens to his body. He learns how to wait. But when his leg returns, everything just picks up where it all left off, as though mocking his anxiety.

The bus comes quickly and he gets on with a quick pivot of the stick. He walks confidently down the aisle to find a window seat. He notices an open newspaper in the seat ahead. The owner shuffles the pages and Arjun glimpses the headline. 'Charlie is Our Darling!' The photo is of Chaplin with yet another woman. How can they put that kind of gossip in a newspaper? He glances again. The *Daily Mail*.

The rain has cleared up and the sun shines on the still-glistening trees, sparkles on the grass and a large pool of water reflects a still portrait of a betting shop. Umbrellas have been furled and raincoats have been daringly unbuttoned. There is a sense of freedom in the sunshine, warm and welcome through Arjun's window.

It is too early for the pubs to be open, but he can imagine what they will be like around lunchtime. If the sunshine persists, perhaps people will spill out onto the pavement and raise their half-glasses of shandy or lager to each other. *Cheers*. He imagines the women in their office dresses and the men in jackets, ties loosened, everyone full of stories from the morning's business. He would like to hear them laughing and talking in that energetic way of the young.

Suddenly someone plops into the seat next to him. A young girl settles herself and says, 'Hello Mr Kulkani.'

Rebecca, fifteen, in a red corduroy dress, clumpy black boots and a multicoloured knitted hat. 'Hello Rebecca. What are you doing here?'

'Just going to the shops.' She pulls her hat off. 'This stupid hat. My mother made me wear it. What do you think? She made it.' She holds it out for him to look at. It is a yellow, red and black eyesore. He wants to say the correct thing, *It was very nice of her*, but the hat is so angrily ugly.

'Does your mother enjoy knitting?'

'What do *you* think?'

'Well. She's a kind person.' His voice wavers a little. Is knitting necessarily a product of kindness?

Rebecca echoes the thought. 'She's not kind. She hates everything.'

She stuffs the hat into the pocket of the black raincoat bundled over her arm. 'Where are you going?'

'The hospital. For tests.'

'Oh, right. So, what are the tests for?'

'My leg. It keeps going out. As you may remember.'

They make eye contact and the laughter trips out of him. Rebecca laughs too, rubs the back of her hand across her mouth. 'You should have seen my mother's face. She looked like she'd been electrocuted.'

'It was terrible.' He tries not to laugh again.

'It was the funniest thing I've seen in ages. She was holding her boobs like they were the crown jewels.'

Rebecca is a fizzy drink of energy; she flaps her hands about, opens her eyes wide, rocks forward. She stops laughing and looks down. 'Still, that's bad luck. Your leg.'

'Oh, it's been happening for a while. It's probably nothing.' He wonders what it's like to be that age again, to feel all that vitality rushing through the body. He remembers back in India when he would start running full tilt up the hill to the school: the sheer exhilaration and strength of his body.

Rebecca touches his arm. 'I'm coming with you.'

'That's very nice of you, but aren't you—?'

'This won't be much of a detour.'

He doesn't want this red-haired young girl with orange fingernails to accompany him into the specialist's office, to witness the bored sympathy, the formulaic kindness. More than that, he doesn't want a witness to his disease being handed to him with a follow-up appointment card. He is quite prepared to lie to Sunila. *Just a bit of muscle fatigue, the doctor said.*

But Rebecca stands up. 'My dad says when I've made up my mind, there's no stopping me. This is our stop. Come on, Mr Kulkani. It could be worse. It could be my mother.'

They walk through the hospital gates and along the path between the spindly rhododendron bushes. The red and brown building looks ancient. He wishes it was metal and glass and modern, with the promise of new medication and advanced treatment.

'Do you watch *The Partridge Family*, Mr Kulkani? I watch it round my friend's house. David Cassidy's *so* dishy. I want to get my hair feathered like his. You won't tell Mum, will you?'

'What? No.' They approach the automatic doors. The left one swings wide, the right tags along afterwards as though it isn't sure it wants to open.

'Anyway, last week—'

'Rebecca, I really appreciate you coming in with me, but I think it will be better if I do this alone.'

She purses a mouth unevenly caulked with red lipstick, probably applied as she was walking away from her home. 'I can get you a cup of tea while you're waiting.'

He hands his piece of paper to the receptionist and they are directed to a waiting room. 'You'll be called shortly.'

'We all know what that means.' Rebecca leads the way, her boots squeaking as if she is squashing mice with each step.

The waiting room is a faded wash of peach. A few old people have settled into the stuffed chairs like elderly pot plants. Rebecca selects a deep, soft-looking chair with a black velvet cushion and offers it to him.

'Thank you, Rebecca.' He dislikes these soft chairs, but doesn't like to refuse her.

She pulls her own chair closer to his. 'Fancy some tea?'

'No, thank you.' He clears his throat. 'So, Rebecca, how are you doing at school?'

A scornful look. 'School?'

A nurse comes in. 'Mr Kulkani? Come this way, please.'

He stands up and collects his cane while the nurse taps her clipboard against her leg. He turns at the doorway. 'Please don't wait, Rebecca. I don't know how long this will take.'

She's looking down at her boots, her hair masking her face. He hopes she has heard.

He follows the nurse, expecting to be taken into a doctor's office, but he is deposited in another waiting room.

'Wait here. They'll call you in a minute.' The nurse walks away.

The second waiting room is smaller with fewer magazines, but the chairs are more padded. This might be a bad sign. He examines them. Are there indentations, signs of long occupancy?

Just as he is considering whether it's worth sitting down, another nurse arrives and takes him to a small office. The impression is of stepping into a boat: blue-painted walls and the ceiling wavering with light reflected from a long fish tank set against the window. He sits in the hard-backed chair and prepares to listen to the doctor's attempt to diagnose him.

'Let's see what we have here. Well, Mr Kulkani, this motor neurone history in your family and your tests appear to confirm what I thought.' Dr Artunian, a young man in his early thirties, settles his glasses. 'Probably spinal muscular atrophy. Probably.' He looks up, the words floating between them. Arjun doesn't want to say anything that indicates he accepts this nebulous sentence. Even though he's guessed for years, carried the self-diagnosis around at the back of his mind, he still feels the emotional rush. *Not that.* Not the slow rot of muscle, the lapse of response, the body's retreat from the will.

'Yes. That's what I thought.' The words barely make it out of his mouth. Did he actually say anything?

He remembers when he worked as a nurse, comforting patients also condemned to long, relentless diseases. He sat next to their beds, listening to their fears that their wives wouldn't be able to take care of them, that their children would be too afraid for hugs, that they would turn into that hell of *being a burden*. He sat and listened long after he should have been off-duty.

But this barely qualified doctor doesn't want to wait for more than the five minutes he has allotted to Arjun. How can a young active man, who has no personal knowledge of the reality of his theory, be qualified to pass on this information?

'I'm fairly sure it's SMA, but we'll schedule more tests to confirm. Let's set you up for next week, Mr Kulkani.' He hits a buzzer on the desk and talks rapidly into a speaker. He turns back to Arjun. 'I'll have more information after I see the results. That's it for now, Mr Kulkani.'

Arjun is irritated with the way his name is repeated, as though the doctor is afraid it will escape and keeps hauling it back by its tail. He stands up. 'Thank you, doctor.'

'The nurse will see to you. You can go down to the desk and they'll make your appointment. Do you hike?'

Arjun has a vision of himself in leather shorts and hiking boots, trudging around the local shops.

'Get some exercise. Move those leg muscles. You don't want to lose any more, do you?'

Arjun is insulted. Move those leg muscles, indeed. He clears his throat and summons a cursory note. 'Yes. I see.'

'Older patients are more susceptible to muscle atrophy.'

Older? Muscle atrophy? Arjun cannot speak: he, a former member of the Maharashtra Squash Racquets Team to be spoken to as though he is an ignorant, ageing fool?

The doctor is already out of his office and walking along the corridor. Arjun follows, trying to adjust his pace to this impatient young idiot's.

The doctor smacks Arjun's file on the receptionist's desk. 'Let's have Mr Kulkani set up for tests. I've given Mercedes the details.' He raps the desk with his knuckles and waves a cautionary finger. 'Walking, Mr Kulkani. It's good for you.' He strides off.

Arjun is winded as much by the brevity of the consultation as the doctor's peremptory manner, wagging his finger as though Arjun is a naughty child.

The nurse writes his test appointment on a piece of card and hands it over.

'Does he always treat his patients so – so—'

The nurse lowers her voice. 'Dr Artunian? He's all right. A bit short sometimes.' She pulls a face.

'I came in for a consultation and he barely spoke to me.'

'He wants to wait for the test results.'

'I wanted to discuss this idea of muscular spinal atrophy. You see, I'm familiar with the symptomology.'

'Symptomology? You *said* that?' The nurse's eyes are round.

'I just—'

'Mr Kulkani, a word to the wise. As far as Dr Artunian is concerned, you're the patient and he's the doctor. Remember that and you'll be fine.' She smiles at him and turns to answer the phone.

Really, does Artunian think he's the only one with medical training? There are a number of Arjun's Air Force experiences that would certainly open that young idiot's eyes. Arjun is nearly at the lifts when he remembers Rebecca. She has probably waited for him, and it won't do to meet her while he is so unsettled. He decides to walk back along the corridor a little way.

The usual display of ridiculous tepid pictures. But perhaps they will help him to calm down. He is not calm. This is an interesting discovery. He has been used to practising calm over the years as a defence against Sunila's volatile moods. He is practised enough that people often turn to him. *Arjun has a level head. Let's see what he thinks. You can always rely on him for a sensible opinion.*

Well, he doesn't feel sensible now. Strange internal surgings make him stop and breathe more deeply. With joyful recognition, he realizes he is angry.

He stands in front of the first picture. It is a pastel, like all hospital pictures, as if the administration doesn't wish to shock people into exacerbated conditions. A red boat sails endlessly on a placid ocean. He snorts. What rubbish. If this were real life, the boat would be drab brown and hung with mended fishing nets. The sea might be placid, but the sky would be a sick yellow.

There are no people in the picture. In reality, there would be dark figures with wiry arms and legs, hauling in the dribbling of a useless catch. Their faces would be scored with sun, their arms and legs and backs running with sweat. The water would be the colour of pewter.

Older patients. He breathes in a vivifying draught of anger and walks on to the next picture. This one is the same, but it includes a peach-coloured strip of sand, a white-and-blue-striped umbrella over a white wooden beach chair. It is such a useless painting that he begins to laugh. He doesn't know if he is laughing at the painting, the doctor or himself.

He catches his breath and hears another gasp. He turns around, surprised and pleased to find that someone else sees the humour in the so-called artwork. No one is in the corridor. Nearby, a doorway leads into another waiting room and he walks over to look in.

A woman stands by the far window. She is in three-quarters profile. He sees that she is dressed beautifully, and she is weeping. One hand grips the windowsill and the other holds a handkerchief over her mouth.

She must be in her late forties? Early fifties? Her hair is lovely: silver with light brown streaks. She has a small straight nose and dark brown eyebrows. He wonders if she is an actress.

Clearly she wants to be alone. Under normal circumstances, he might not even have hesitated at the doorway, but his anger propels him through.

'I have been examining the pictures.'

She looks up, startled.

'They are an abomination. An absolute abomination. No one wants to look at pink beaches and fishing boats. It's time they stopped putting up this remedial nonsense. Perhaps paintings by children. At least that would be more interesting.' He says, 'Arjun Kulkani at your service.'

The old-fashioned words have an effect. She smiles. 'Marlene Varga.'

'Pleased to meet you, Mrs Varga.' He bows slightly. 'And how are the gardens?' He joins her at the window. 'Aha. As I thought. A sad state. Why do hospitals think that they must always plant rhododendrons?'

She says, 'Just what I was thinking. So many rhododendrons.' Her accent is barely distinguishable.

'What this place needs is dahlias and peonies. Lots of colour. And sunflowers.'

A gentle smile. 'Sunflowers. I so love this yellow and black combination.'

'I planted some in my garden a few years back.'

'And did they grow?'

'They grew, but they didn't flower. I had all these ten-foot stalks and not one flower.'

She laughs. 'I can just imagine that. How disappointing. I very much like these small white flowers.'

'Jasmine?'

'They are a winter flower with the scent of a lemon. It is a longer name than jasmine.'

He runs through the names of white winter flowers. 'Clematis?'

'Ah, yes! Clematis. My neighbour has some and they grow over my fence. And I can stand underneath and look up at them.'

He inhales too, imagining the smell of flowers he has only seen in the gardening catalogue.

A young voice crashes into the room. 'There you are, Mr Kulkani. I've been looking all over for you.' Rebecca, in her thick boots and rumpled dress, smiles at him. 'So, who's this?'

He clears his throat. 'Mrs Varga, this is Rebecca. She is the daughter of one of my church friends.'

Mrs Varga says, 'I am pleased to meet you, Rebecca.'

Rebecca is too loud for the room. 'I'm just taking care of Mr Kulkani. I'll have to put him back on the bus now.' She says this as though he is some doddering idiot who might wander off in his nightshirt.

Mrs Varga says, 'How good it is to have friends.'

Rebecca stands with her hands on her hips. 'Ready, then?'

'Mrs Varga, I have to go now. It was a pleasure to talk to you.' He half-bows to her, aware that Rebecca is watching him.

They walk out of the hospital, Rebecca pressing lift buttons, opening doors, assuring him that they'll soon be out of this place.

It's colder now, the promise of a warm day gone. Rebecca pulls her knitted hat on. She looks even younger.

'What did she want, then?'

'Who? Oh, Mrs Varga. She didn't want anything.'

'She wasn't a nurse. Who was she?'

'A patient, probably.'

'Just came up to you, did she? Well. You're a bit of a dark horse, even if you are old.'

He wants to protest. *It wasn't like that. We talked about flowers. And forty-three isn't old.*

But she's right, of course. He's been flirting. And this child saw it.

'I've got David Cassidy and you've got Mrs Varga.' Rebecca nudges him. 'It's all right. Your secret's safe with me, Mr Kulkani.'

On the bus, Rebecca talks about how difficult life is with her mother. Arjun nods sympathetically for this, too, is a need for attention, for a little love.

He imagines Mrs Varga standing under the white bell-like flowers, her face turned up, eyes closed as she inhales the

fragrance. He inhales Rebecca's overpowering perfume
and coughs it out quickly.

Mercifully, she is persuaded to stay on the bus and he
is relieved to wave her off. The momentary elation over
his flirting has worn off and the half-mile home feels
much longer.

Sunila has left the front door unlocked and comes
hurrying out into the hall.

'What did they say?'

'Nothing conclusive. Tests in two weeks.'

There is a faint chemical smell and he sniffs to detect
the source. He glances at Sunila's hands. She has painted
her nails rose pink. She curls her fingers under. 'I thought
I'd do something to pass the time.'

'It looks nice.' His voice goes up and down uneasily.
Her fingers are short and her thick, ribbed nails aren't
disguised by the nail polish.

Suddenly he feels a longing shift and tilt its anchor
inside him, and his age settles into his bones. The lift of
a pretty smile, the chance to spread creaking wings and
the illusion of flight when in fact all he has done is resettle
on his perch.

Gradually the leg will function less and less and,
eventually, the other leg too. He looks down at his right
hand, extends the fingers. What will it be like not to
hold a squash racquet, to fire back a return or aim an
unreturnable shot? His feet are rooted firmly on the hallway
carpet. His body fills the space there, strong and present.

What will it be like not to stand like this? Has he become someone else over the course of a couple of hours during this hospital visit? He will go out of the house tomorrow, walk along the road to catch the bus, sit in the train and stride up the steps to the office. Even now he knows this thing is already moving inside him, switching off neurons like unnecessary lights.

Sunila says, 'Cup of tea, then?'

'Yes, please.'

8

NO CURE

APRIL 1973

Tarani deftly wraps two bottles of mango pickle in green tissue paper. Sunila admires the slender fingers, the quick movements. Such a shame. She's sixteen and she still bites her nails.

Tarani dumps the money into the small moneybox. 'Mrs Singh's pickle-oo is going like the blazes, yes please?'

Sunila laughs at the Indian accent, then whispers, 'Don't let Mrs Singh hear you. She'll think you're making fun of her.'

'What-what-what? Making fun only? How dare you!' Tarani mimics the small woman with caterpillar eyebrows. 'Sorry, Mum. I'll behave.' She shakes the moneybox. 'Look, the aunties' pillows, bed sheets and floor cushions are sold out and it's not even ten.'

Haseena and Nawal's business has come a long way from lavender sachets. Three days a week they wear long white aprons embroidered with 'H&N' as they work behind a counter on one side of Pritty's Flower Shop in Hounslow. The window has a small display of soaps, pressed-flower cards and decorated picture frames. Inside, there is a tasteful arrangement of cushions, crocheted blankets, satin bed sheets and even plastic placemats with lavender buds inside. Sunila bet against those. Who would want a lumpy placemat? But the women in Hounslow can't get enough of lavender. The commissions have started to come in for monogrammed down quilts, table runners and wedding-party favours. *So exotic, so tasteful.*

Sunila tells herself that she is happy for Haseena and Nawal, but she is hurt. Sunila has always been good with flowers. The women at church ask for her flower arrangements and she willingly gives them away. Why didn't Haseena and Nawal ask for her help? She could have suggested hundreds of ideas for the lavender, and her pressed-flower cards would have been much more colourful. Nawal's are merely leaves and a few flowers with some kind of ink flourish that is meant to look 'Eastern'. At a deeper level, Sunila admits that she would have liked to be involved in a family business, something she could take pride in. She imagines her name on the flyers and business cards: HN&S. Almost like M&S. What style and cachet she could have brought to the shop.

Well, no use crying over what's not going to happen. She looks around the church hall. The women are comfortably chatting at their neatly ordered tables of cakes and pies, jams and jellabies, relishes and samosas, handmade chocolates and braided breads. There's a scented goodwill in the air as they recite recipes and complain about their children, who pester them for whatever is being sold here at Hounslow Evangelical.

Tarani hugs Sunila. 'Mum, are you okay? I'm just joking with you. You British are so uptight.'

It's an old joke and one that Sunila can now endure. Tarani doesn't see herself as British any more. She's begun to claim her Indian side with an enthusiasm that is slightly repulsive. But perhaps that's because Tarani has had an easier time than Murad, who still rejects any suggestion that he is Indian. Tarani only had a fraction of the name-calling and teasing Murad had to go through at school.

Murad is resitting his S-level chemistry, but it doesn't look like he'll score high enough for Cardiff University. Tarani, a year away from her A-level exams, is sailing through economics, maths and English. Sunila mourns Murad, the firstborn, the beloved son and centre of her life. Meanwhile, Tarani, suddenly a young woman, ignores the tragedy of Murad's exam results and scandalizes her father with blue eyeshadow, big, clumping boots and red glittery skintight trousers.

As if trying to insult everyone at once, Tarani renounced last year's family holiday and took her glittery trousers and yellow boots to Paris with her friend, Edwidge. It was hurtful that Tarani preferred Edwidge and her museum-mad parents. There were plenty of museums in London.

And what was wrong with a nice trip to Weston-super-Mare? Where this travel bug comes from Sunila still doesn't know. It isn't proper how the young hop from one country to another, seeking who knows what, mingling with foreigners who speak all kinds of gobbledygook. Where is the normal life she once believed was possible for her children?

'Did you see those loony people at the corner?' Tarani is peering out of the window facing the street.

'Come away from the window. Someone will see you.'

'Mum, you've got to see this.' Tarani beckons and Sunila finds herself gazing out at the peaceful drift of the clouds, the broccoli crowns of the trees and a brown spaniel trotting busily along in front of a young man.

By the traffic light, two girls and one boy each hold a yellow banner printed with black lettering. *Trust in Christ, Jesus is the Answer* and *Pray Each Day and Give Thanks*. Sunila is indignant. Who are these people to walk around advertising Jesus like He's a carpet sale?

Tarani shakes her head. 'It's such a lovely day. I want to go out there and hand them a few pounds, tell them, "Go to an art exhibition".'

'There's more to life than swanning around art exhibitions. At least they love Jesus.'

'Oh, come on, Mum. If you were to go up and ask them what their banners meant, they wouldn't know what to say. I mean, they're *beyond*.' Tarani turns back to the table.

'I think it's perfectly clear what it means to trust in Christ,' Sunila mutters. Her voice sounds stiff and old.

Beyond. Is this what the young say these days? Isn't that disrespectful?

'Mango pickle? Absolutely. Here we go.' Tarani wraps a bottle of pickle and smiles at a young couple.

Sunila waits until they have left. Is this the opportunity she's so longed for? Can she lead Tarani into a calm discussion about giving her heart to Christ? 'Well, you're probably right. But asking people to give thanks and pray isn't such a terrible thing, is it?'

Tarani looks up from counting the change. 'Sorry, Mum?'

'Giving thanks. You know.'

Too many arguments have made Sunila wary of her daughter, who can say such careless, cruel things about God. How can Tarani remain so resistant to the call? If she could only see how God takes care of everything. Even for this trip to Hounslow, God sent the bus on time. It could easily have been late and they wouldn't have been able to help in setting up the tables. Sunila, the wife of an elder, can't just sit back and take things easy. Not like Mrs Hargreve, the poor darling, who sits about and waits for everything to be done. Sunila allows herself to think of other pleasures: church mornings when she graciously accepts congratulations on her flower arrangements from the other church women; when Pastor Hargreve warmly shakes her hand; when she kindly permits Mrs Hargreve her choice of the arrangements, although she always picks the one with the most roses. Is Mrs Hargreve *beyond*?

'I'll get us a cup of tea, shall I, Mum?'

'Lovely.'

Sunila watches her daughter squeeze between people like a little woodland creature. Well, perhaps not a woodland creature. That sounds too dark and Tarani is quite light. If they were in India, and thank God they aren't, they could quite truthfully advertise her as wheat-complexioned. Some of those marriage ads are such nonsense. Wheat-complexioned, indeed, when the girl is as black as coal. The nerve of some people.

Tarani arrives back, holding the teacups up like raffle prizes. Sunila smiles brightly at her daughter. 'Bless you. You brought biscuits as well.'

'Chocolate. Mrs Hargreve gave me a funny look when I took four but I smiled at her sweetly. There was a whole plateful, and it's not like I took the last ones.' Tarani settles one cup in front of Sunila.

Sunila can't help a smile at the thought. 'I'm sure it's perfectly okay, darling.'

'Nice cuppa.' Tarani sips appreciatively. 'Not like Paris. They love their coffee but you can't find a decent cup of tea.'

Sometimes Sunila suspects that her daughter brings up Paris just to be irritating. What can Sunila say about the quality of tea or coffee in Paris?

Tarani puts her tea down and shuffles her chair closer to Sunila. 'Has Murad made a decision yet?'

Sunila rotates the cup in the saucer. 'Not yet.' An Australian couple at the church have invited Murad to come with them back to Cairns and try out their tourist-guide business. *Just for a change of pace.*

Tarani bites into a McVitie's. 'Lots of people are going over. Edwidge's older sister just took a job in Melbourne.'

'And why should Murad go guiding tourists around? What does he know about Australia?'

'It's a chance for him—' Tarani falters and stops.

Sunila nods and speaks quietly. 'He's still disappointed about the first S-level, you know. It was a terrible blow.'

'Mum, Murad's really clever. He can retake again. He'll do well.'

'Even so. You don't know your brother. He was always a sensitive child.'

'He's nineteen.'

Sunila rotates the cup. 'It's not really this S-level business. Of course he could pass this time. It was the rejection from Cardiff.'

'He can still go to uni, Mum. Sussex offered him a place already. They don't need an S-level.'

'But the programme at Cardiff is so much better. He knows about these things. He researched it all up in the library.' Sunila feels her eyes beginning to water. 'He wanted it so much.'

'I know. Well.' Tarani scratches an ear. 'This job in Australia sounds great. *I'd* go.'

Sunila sighs. 'Not everyone is like you, child. He can't just rush off to the other side of the world because someone offers him a job. He's more thoughtful about these things.' Sunila grips the saucer. Calm, calm, calm.

'Mum, are you still upset about Paris?'

'You just don't think sometimes, Tarani. We'd made plans.'

'To go to Weston-super-Mare?'

'Your father was planning to take time off specially.'

'Mum, we can *always* go to Weston-super-Mare. This was *Paris*.'

'You'll have plenty of chances to go anywhere you want. But you had to go *right now*. Everything is *right now* with you. Not a thought for the rest of us.' She manages to keep her voice down, although she can feel herself beginning to tremble. How she hates this kind of talk. If only she and Tarani could just get along better.

'I'm tired of staying at home all the time.'

'What "all the time"? We went to Cheddar Gorge only last year.'

'I want to go somewhere *else*. Somewhere abroad. I loved Paris. I even managed to say some things in French.'

Sunila is unmoved. What's wrong with speaking English? All these years she's avoided speaking Hindi so that her children could have a pure British upbringing and now her daughter wants to start gabbling in some foreign language.

'You can go anywhere you want when you're older.'

'How much older do I have to be? Look at you – you came all the way from India to England. That must have been amazing.'

How to explain the sheer relief of leaving India for England? But she'd suffered for it. The cramped voyage in third class, the embarrassment of being sick the whole time, how she prayed to stay alive for those three horrible weeks. Back then, travel was a necessary evil. How can Tarani enjoy it? Sunila feels like she has nurtured some kind of cuckoo.

'It was different. It wasn't all fun and games.' She wobbles one foot, trying to release the argument anxiety. 'Anyway, your brother feels there are more important things to consider than just some hare-brained scheme.'

'Murad is afraid. That's why he won't do anything. But this chemistry S-level isn't the end of the world. And anyway, he passed *five* exams. That's more than most people.'

Sunila suddenly remembers Tarani's sullen face when she had to help cook dinners for guests, to hand around the food, to wash the dishes afterwards. *Why can't Murad do it?* It was no use telling her that boys didn't do these things. Tarani rebelled against going to church, against playing the flute or even being polite to guests. Arjun, unable to handle the rude outbursts or the sarcasm that he was unable to beat out of her, stopped trying to talk to her. Murad, for all his silences, was never rude.

'Murad cares about his family.' Sunila feels heroic, not saying what she really wants to say, resisting the old impulse to slap this selfish child's face to bring her to her senses.

'I care too. It's just that I don't want to stay in north London for ever.'

A chord of agreement that Sunila hopes isn't apparent. She, too, hoped for something else. Richmond, Kew, even Hemel Hempstead with its proximity to St Albans. Hayes with its small inadequate shops was never how she imagined England.

'I can't stand being around Dad.'

Sunila gasps. 'Tarani, you can't speak like this.'

Tarani looks a little dazed. She looks down, as though the words have fallen in between the linoleum's brown leaf pattern. 'I'm sorry, Mum. I'll get us another cup of tea.' She picks up both cups and walks away.

Sunila watches Tarani slide between a checked raincoat and a purple cardigan. The purple cardigan is determinedly making for the table. 'Ah, Sunila, lovely to see you. Your table's doing *so* well.'

'Thank you, Mary.'

'Weld.' Bright smile.

'I'm sorry. Maryweld.'

'Bit of a mouthful for some people. Not popular these days. All these Katies and Julies and I don't know what. Still. Maryweld. I always know where I am with that name.'

Sunila smiles.

'So, Sunila, I've always meant to ask. What does *your* name mean? I know you people love to give meaningful names.'

'It was my grandmother's name.'

'Ah yes. Family history. I'm a bit of a dab hand at that. Now, for instance, my family, the Kembles, go back to the twelfth century, or so I'm told.' A little laugh. 'The old English is quaint. Cynbel. Isn't that lovely? I'm doing a genealogical chart.'

'How clever of you.'

'Everything's verified, of course. So.' Maryweld finally pauses for breath and leans on the edge of the table. 'I can't believe the Duchess of Windsor's gone, can you?'

It's only a card table and not capable of bearing much weight. Sunila tries to think of something tactful to say. 'I never really thought of her as royalty.'

'Me either. Bit of an upstart, really, wasn't she? But beautiful. You can see why he went for her. The prince. I must say, if some prince came along and offered himself—'

A noise like a gunshot and the table shudders, tilts and collapses. The remaining pickles and small bottles of ghee slide sideways, taking a startled-looking Maryweld with them.

To her shame, Sunila's first thought is for the broken bottles and the wasted food. After that, there is the real danger of injury, but Maryweld appears unhurt.

The unmistakably pungent smell of mango pickle and the Hounslow church hall is magically transported to a Bombay market, stall owners hustling mangoes, pineapples, *chaat*, chicken tandoori. The bhel-puri man is grinding up the tamarind and you can almost catch the sweet scents of jaggery and mint.

'My goodness. *What* a smell.' Maryweld has been helped into a chair.

Pastor Hargreve arrives, followed by someone with a broom. 'Is everyone all right? Mrs Kulkani, can I trouble you to move a little?'

'It was the table, you see,' Sunila starts to explain.

'Don't worry about it, Mrs K. These tables are so ancient I'd expect to find fossils embedded in them.'

'Well, *I* almost was.' Maryweld is indignant.

'My dear Maryweld, no one would consider you a fossil.' The pastor is pleased with his joke and Maryweld roars with laughter. Sunila smiles anxiously and moves away. Perhaps she should find a bucket and mop to help clear up. Was it her fault? Should she have been quicker to stop Maryweld from leaning on the table? And what if Maryweld had been cut by the broken glass?

'Are you okay? What happened?' Tarani, holding two cups of tea. She puts them down on the nearest table.

Sunila can't help the tears pricking. So foolish.

'Come on, Mum, let's get some fresh air.'

Sunila allows Tarani to lead her out into the foyer where the coats, piled two or three deep, tent the hooks. Beneath is a wooden bench.

'It's a bit cold outside. We'll stay here.' Tarani sits next to her. 'Oh, Mum. It's all right,' she says, and hugs Sunila as she cries her stupid tears.

Sunila pulls out a handkerchief and wipes her eyes. 'I'm sorry, darling. It just happened. She leant on the table and it collapsed. *Buthuk*. Just like that.'

There is a trembling and for a moment Sunila thinks that Tarani is also crying. But she looks up to see her daughter shaking with laughter. 'It's funny?'

'Oh, Mum. *Buthuk*. Just like Uncle Jonti used to say.'

Sunila laughs a little, too.

'It was just an accident. And the old bat wasn't hurt.' Tarani takes the tissue from Sunila and wipes the tears.

'You shouldn't call her that. She's just, you know—'

'Boring. Her family this and her lineage that.'

'She's lonely, Tarani. She has no one at home, poor thing. No children. She hasn't even got a cat or a dog.'

'She'd bore it to death.' Tarani smiles at her. 'Okay, I'm just kidding.' She laughs again. 'Just as well Dad wasn't here. Can you imagine? Him with his leg and Maryweld on top!'

'Tarani, don't speak about him like that.'

'He fell downstairs at the weekend. You were at Pavi Aunty's.'

'Was he hurt?' Why hadn't he told her?

'He laughed.'

And for a moment it's possible to see it: they are the family with someone who falls down. Then they pick him up and they all laugh about it, lovingly. And they carry on. Everything is normal again.

They sit comfortably, leaning against the coats.

'What you said about Dad.'

'I didn't mean it, Mum.'

'I know. But he really does love you. And he's very proud of you. I know you've had your differences. But all he's ever wanted is for you and Murad to be happy here. He felt it was his responsibility to make that happen.'

'Come on, Mum, you must remember.'

And Sunila does. *You're just a little Indian girl. No one will take a second look at you. Girls can't do the same things as boys. You have to remember, you're a second-class person.*

Her heart jumps against the back of her ribs. 'You don't know what it was like for him. His own father hated him so much that they used to send the servant to meet him from school to tell him to stay at his grandmother's. Because if he came home, his father would beat him senseless.'

'What?'

'Your grandfather used to drink this Indian whisky. Filthy stuff. Then beat your dad and lock him in the chicken coop under the house. They left him there all night. He was only seven. And his mother wasn't much better.'

'Grandma?'

'He got dressed up to go to a school dance once and she caught hold of him and stripped him naked for the others to laugh at. Monkey boy, she called him.'

'*Why?*'

Sunila hesitates. She has a half-theory. Arjun, the unwanted child who arrived four months after the forced wedding. This was a whispered secret from Jonti. *So you can understand why he is sometimes a little impatient. No one showed him any patience.*

'It was just like that.' Sunila sits up. 'Don't you *ever* say anything about this. Not to anyone.'

Almost every day, she wakes up relieved and grateful to be in England but, even now, after more than nineteen years, she doesn't have that careless ease of her children's British mannerisms and ways of talking. They are so at home here.

Sometimes Murad talks to her, late in the evenings, telling over the story of his S-level chemistry exam. She has no British advice to give, but reminds him gently, 'God will heal your heart, son.' Well, this Australia business will soon be over and he still might pass this year and get into Cardiff.

She wonders what Arjun would make of this, she and Tarani sitting together and holding hands. He looks puzzled when he sees his daughter these days. Who is this young woman who once ran after him in her nappies and bossed him about?

Poor Arjun. Once upon a time she loved him and trusted him to bring her to England. A strict father, but he only wanted the best for the kids. And look at them all now: Tarani so bitter and Murad so resentful. And she, Sunila, wondering how it is that she no longer loves her husband. What is love, anyway? Just a song with a pretty tune. No one ever mentions that love comes with a fist to the back, a hand around the throat.

No matter. No matter. She squeezes Tarani's hand. One thing is certain: this is her daughter. This is her child. She can do nothing else but love her.

PART II

9

TREMORS WHEN THE PATIENT'S HANDS ARE HELD OUT

MARCH 1998

They have grown into each other like two sun-exhausted creepers; a combination of indistinct markings. An outsider might wonder if these are the original patterns, or if there has been some constant irritation to produce this blurring together of striation.

Once they were young and strong enough to stand with stiff shoulders. They never looked at one another except to grieve that the other was still there. *You*, their eyes said as they snapped themselves apart like press-studs.

Their children have gone into other lives. Tarani, now forty-one, is living in Boston. Sunila is relieved; at least it's not India. Until this year, when Tarani became pregnant, Arjun didn't speak to her much. He knew she disliked him when she was growing up, but she seems to like him now. Maybe the anxiety of a late pregnancy has softened her. Arjun believes that a lot of people dislike him for reasons he will never understand. He lets his small hesitancies drop here and there, like elderly rose petals.

Murad left England for Cairns, Australia, to work as a tourist guide. He is now forty-four. *Just imagine,* Sunila with her palm to her cheek. A grown man, slightly more than middle-aged, even. He owns a kayaking shop, whatever that is. His accent changed: a gradual lengthening of vowels as though he stretched into another culture. It takes some adjustment of the ears to speak to him on the phone when he calls from this other world. They marvel at their once silent child's business acumen suddenly flowering in a strange, hot place where they have Wollemi pines, tea trees, mud crabs and something called a queenfish.

They show their visitors the map of Australia in the *World Atlas*. Cairns is an orange smudge on page seventy-six and the sea next to it is a rich, deep blue. The visitors admire the colour combination and note the Great Barrier Reef. Arjun and Sunila nod proudly as though Murad owns the Great Barrier Reef too.

They feel they ought to be more entertaining, but have lost the energy. They look about as if the energy might be lying under sofa cushions, or snagged on curtain hooks.

They talk about their children much more now that they are gone. It is the way of parents. They argue with barely enough energy to contradict each other. Sunila

remembers Tarani's hair was long. Arjun recalls it was
short. He knows this is so since it shocked him. He had
not thought she would ever get her hair cut so short. He
shakes his head wonderingly; it was as though she had
suddenly changed sex. When she visits, he marvels at how
it's grown long again.

Even now they fight each other with their exhaustion.
Arjun wills himself to wake at six, to crumble into clothes
as fast as his disobedient hands will let him. He can do very
little alone. Soon he will do less and Sunila will be forced
to bathe him, take him to the toilet. She will wonder how
long she can keep it up, this attendance on every little
thing he wants.

The early spring sun shows petulantly behind breaking
clouds as they walk slowly to the local shops; Arjun with
his walking frame, Sunila with the pull-along bag. His
walking frame catches on the smallest pebble, the tiniest
crack. A dog ambles by and stops to sniff his shoes. He
is delighted with the insult. 'See this fellow? He has no
respect. Get along with you, you old tramp.' His voice
is fond over this attention. The dog salutes him with a
cocky glance and a half-laugh, coral tongue dragging
out of the left side of its mouth. It trots off, its liver and
white markings jogging under the deep green of the privet
hedges flanking the road.

They have to cross the road to get to the shops. He
tries to move quickly to avoid traffic. Sunila waits on the
far kerb while Arjun takes too long to stumble across the

street to safety. How far it is. Once he would have taken a few strides and confidently stepped up onto the opposite pavement.

There was a time when the mountains were familiar with his quick, tireless stride. There were mountain streams he stepped across. The freezing water slapped against his legs making him gasp as he waded quickly, jumping onto the mud-warm bank.

There was facile movement and no pain. Perhaps this is why so many of the elderly are Christians. A land fairer than day where there is no pain is obviously unreal.

What does she think of, this old woman with the white puffball hair, as she tries to walk slowly so that the husband can keep up? Does she remember how he once moved like a jungle cat across the squash court, the speed and accuracy of his shots, how the crowd gasped when he made a daring snatch at the ball seemingly out of reach? How he used to hold her hand in the cinema in Bombay, how his fingers gently curled around hers? She watches the walker inching along, closer, closer.

As the old man reaches what he now thinks of as the shore, a car turns a nearby corner. He stops to glance at it and the woman bends forward and tugs at him. 'Get up on the pavement before you kill yourself.' She catches him off balance and he stumbles. She drops the pull-along bag and grabs at him, hoisting him onto the pavement. She steadies him and retrieves the walker. She picks up the pull-along and trundles away into the greengrocer's.

The cold air carries traces of car exhaust, something fried and, just barely, the woody smell of the small trees planted alongside the row of shops. Does he think about going into his garden later? Perhaps he might dig in the earth, his fingers loosening the soil. He won't want to plant seeds. The climate is too cold for cacti. His beloved tiger lily, planted in the spring last year, has yet to flower. A succulent? Something pink and green, perhaps. He will think about his succulent, gently lowering it into the soil, adding the water, tamping down the earth around it. His strands of white hair will form antennae in the breeze and his nose will run.

The old woman comes out and beckons the old man to come into the greengrocer's. She wants to know what fruit he wants.

She waits in line behind a huge dyed-blonde perm. The perm turns around and the old woman smiles brightly, says 'Good morning.' The perm cracks a reluctant smile as the greengrocer calls a greeting, asks after the husband. Others also nod and call to the old woman and she happily replies, 'He's doing very well.' The English tolerate immigrants who don't complain.

The old man hears this good news about himself as he inches his way in. They have lived here for forty-four years and have achieved that nodding acquaintance of respectability that has been the woman's life's goal since they arrived in England.

He steadies himself on his walker, smiles his nervous

smile, nods quickly at those who greet him, is grateful to those who overlook him. He would rather be in his garden with the new baby succulent. Perhaps he will talk to the plant as he gently sets its delicate pink and green in the earth.

A small cabbage is set beneath a flourish of carrots under a gaudy display of lights. Since this looks a little like a succulent, the old man turns his nervous smile on it. His smile softens and he transforms the bed of ice around it into dark, moist earth, like Christmas cake. The night stars will look after his succulent, will make sure it's comfortable in its bed, that nothing disturbs it.

The old woman has noticed his glance and gives the grocer her order. The old man watches his baby torn up by the roots. His smile freezes. He will have to eat cabbage. The old woman continues her order: carrots, tomatoes, onions, bananas. Someone says something about a pineapple. The greengrocer says something about Tony Blair. There is laughter.

The old woman enjoys the neighbourly chit-chat, delighted with her idea to make cabbage *fougard* and plain white rice. Pilau is nicer, of course, but more time-consuming.

The old man is still staring at the empty indentation where his succulent once was. He tells himself, *it is only a cabbage*. There is a memory of something else torn away, as though he is an old catalogue. The ice patch has a semicircular impression, a half-smile. Ridicule or regret?

Does he remember that first winter after they arrived in England, when he thought he would lose his toes to frostbite? Or the astonishing lavender mist in the woods as the bluebells came in the spring? Does he remember standing at the children's bedroom door, not wanting to enter in case they awoke? Or how he stood, squinting in the dim light, trying to see whether they looked comfortable, whether the covers were pulled up?

Where has it gone, that quick-firing response of brain to muscle that once made him *himself*, made it possible to see and hear and respond faster than an in-breath? Is the self, then, merely a series of sodium–potassium exchanges? Is there nothing more?

How long the way home is, a type of *Through the Looking-Glass* journey. Roads expand like black plastic, widening each time he must cross. The pavement is steeper each time he must step up, step down. The houses are taller, more shuttered; the grass in each front garden needs cutting. The walker, a shaking birdcage, squeaks its protests as he pushes it forward, stopping at each pavement crack, each new sprout of wild grass poking up between the paving stones.

The old woman is careful to walk slowly so that the old man isn't left too far behind. Once, many years ago, before they left India, there was an argument over whether she should walk behind him, like a good Indian wife. She refused to be a good Indian anything, but at least she is still here.

Perhaps the old man has understood that some curry or stew will be placed in front of him for his enjoyment. But he is not a good actor and she will swipe his plate away and angrily clatter the dishes about in the kitchen. She will complain loudly that nothing she ever does pleases him. He will feel guilty, but a little triumphant that this part of him, what he really likes, remains secret.

The pull-along vanishes around the corner and the old man hesitates by the postbox. How would he reconnect with his children? He might make small jokes about tripping, about falling, about his inability to type an email. Young people don't want to hear about old age. They have their own lives.

Above the postbox, the wires loop between electricity poles, the sliver of a plane needles into the salt-white clouds. The air moves up and beyond, lifts long fingers, stretches out beyond other planes, other electricity poles, descends past autoricks, the fat exhausts of buses, the calls of the rickshaw boys, the chai-wallahs, the paan-wallahs, warms itself around the peanut cart, cools itself around the kulfi ice-cream parlour. Blows itself away to the Great Barrier Reef where Murad guides a boatload of tourists out to the reef; scuds away to a coastal city in America where Tarani lies cradled in the La-Z-Boy waiting for her baby to arrive.

The old woman has walked more quickly past the postbox, a reminder of how they haven't heard from Murad in months. Infrequent news from Tarani, whose phone conversations are interrupted by bouts of morning sickness. The old woman wonders at these children of her flesh who have left. This separation of child and parent is so *foreign*. This would never have happened in India. But, of course, that is exactly what happened. There was a ship that left and a young girl, just married, stood on the third-class deck and threw down a streamer to a small figure in a white sari who bent and caught the paper string and held on to it as though it might be possible to keep her attached, even as the young girl's new world drew her away from the dock. The pull-along is set upright. The white head bends and the old woman pulls her scarf around her face in case anyone is watching, quickly pulls a tissue from her pocket and wipes her eyes.

Is it possible to really know who your children are? The old man wonders why he could never just hug them as they walked past, or touch their hair. He raises his hand, the disobedient fingers clawed together, and brushes the side of his wrist against his balding head.

He wonders what they thought as they pressed their ears against the radio, turned down low. What did they think of their one family vacation abroad to Guernsey? They never said anything; perhaps they hated it. And yet there are photos where they are all smiling. Perhaps it was just one moment, like a squash ball snatched off the side-wall, the moment just before or after the camera flash. He hopes that they are happy, even without him.

The old woman waits by the long low privet hedge at the corner of their road. The sky is partly cloudy, but there is enough blue to make a pair of sailor's trousers. Perhaps it will be sunny after all.

The old man longs for his children to be content. He longs for them to be alone rather than trapped with someone who dislikes them, whom they dislike. Halfway round the world in a place called America, there is a new grandson coming who will know nothing of his grandfather.

He reaches a shaky hand out and touches the top of the postbox, as though he is blessing it.

10

WEAKNESS AND WASTING OF THE VOLUNTARY MUSCLES

APRIL 2000

He is lying in the new hospital bed, just delivered that Sunday morning, when his daughter, Tarani, calls. She's moved back to England after her divorce from the American husband, Hinton. The custody battle is over. She doesn't talk about that. Instead she describes Sami's new bedtime song *(I Bolam, I a puppy, you Tenklu, you a bear)*. She asks how he is adjusting to the bed.

He is no longer able to lie flat on his back; his breathing is difficult. The hospital bed elevates him, although he hates seeing his skinny knees pushed up like thin candles. Also, he can no longer get out of his bed unaided. He used to bring his knees up to his chest and kick to give him the impetus he needed to roll out. But eventually, it didn't work. He could only kick twice and then he was helpless, lying half in, half out, waiting for someone to come and help him. At least the hospital bed permits some dignity of freedom. *Hospital bed*. He resents feeling claimed by the sick and weary, even though he is one of them.

He cannot even ask his god for comfort. This god, who has begun to turn up more frequently, and is often in the room at these moments, is usually examining the prints of elephants or the pictures of Sami. Sometimes he wants to ask, 'So, what good are you?' He knows the answer. He has drawn this god for himself: his black outline, his careful crayons. He's created his own dithery, peripheral god who doesn't have anything else to do because Arjun hasn't assigned him anything. But what room is left when there is Sunila and her now-look-what-you've-done-and-I've-got-to-clean-it-up? Perhaps it's his resistance to any more interfering that has evoked this mellow god who keeps out of the way.

He has told Sunila, 'Don't send me to the hospital. Let me die at home.' He can never get through the second sentence before she crowds his words. 'You're not going to die. You'll live a long while yet.' He is irritated with her inability to face death. After all, it's his death.

It isn't the hospital smell, the indifferent care of the hospital nurses, the barely concealed boredom of the doctors; it is the fact that he would not recognize anything there. He wouldn't have his pictures of Sami, beloved two-year-old grandson, or Sami's creations: a portrait of

Arjun that is blotches of black with spidery arms and legs, the strange brown blob declared a teddy bear, the object made of sticks liberally smattered with glitter glue that is, according to Sami, the moon.

Arjun would miss his back-garden window. He can still reach it if he takes his time, carefully balancing his weight on his walker so that he won't suddenly tip backwards or sideways. He can stand there for a few minutes and gaze at the budding blue fir, or the grass that will soon need cutting, or the valiant green stalks of his tiger lily. Surely this year it will bloom.

Arjun enjoys seeing this abundance of green life pushing up through the soil. He smiles at the wayward dandelions that raise their yellow-tufted heads. Sunila will murder them later, carefully pouring on a solution that will turn them brown. The bright yellow heads remind him of his grandson's spiky black hair. He is secretly pleased that Tarani cannot comb or gel the renegade hair flat. Let Sami defy convention; let him run wildly over the carefully kept garden, Sunila pursuing him and exhorting him not to stand on the new plants, Tarani in her stiletto shoes, shouting pointless threats from the kitchen doorway.

Let Sami tear up the new lemon basil and bring handfuls back for his grandfather to smell. Meanwhile, Sunila will complain and Tarani will roll her eyes. Boys are so destructive. But he will bury his nose into Sami's offering and smile into the bright face. Yes, it smells wonderful. 'S'kee, 'Ampa?' Yes, let's have some ice cream. The dancing light of Sami's energy is surely regenerating his own. Sometimes he feels some urgency moving in him, feels he can almost stand up without the walker, feels something widening his lungs. Surely the muscles will respond for his grandson. He will go to the freezer himself.

But they don't have ice cream. Sunila doesn't approve of ice cream and won't have it in the house. She claims she forgets, but he knows she hates ice cream. It makes her fat, so no one can have it. She is an old woman. Why should she care if she doesn't have an hourglass figure? Old women are for hugging, but Sunila hugs no one. She even hugs Sami carefully, not allowing more than his face to press to hers briefly, something Arjun will not forgive. He would give a good deal to hug his grandson.

The clear flute of Sami's voice opens everything as he pushes through the front door. Tarani follows in his wake, cautioning, hushing, attempting to suppress his bright voice. *Ah? Ah?*

Sami crushes his head against Arjun's chest, then plants a soggy kiss on his cheek.

Arjun is joyful. 'I'm so happy to see you, Sami.'

'S'kee?'

Sunila says, 'Oh dear. I forgot to get some.'

Sami looks at his grandfather.

'Never mind, son, you can get some from the van when it comes by.'

'That van never comes here any more. I don't know what happened to it.' Sunila laughs.

Not even an hour later, the tinkling of 'Greensleeves' announces the van and Sunila has to hide her disapproval and cough up the money for an ice-cream cone.

'Get one with a chocolate flake, son.' Arjun hopes Sami has heard him as he runs to the door, Tarani following on precarious spiked heels shouting about the traffic and holding hands.

Arjun mutters to himself, 'She'll break her neck in those shoes.'

'It's about time she bought something nice for herself. She never had anything from that good-for-nothing man.' Sunila doesn't approve of the shoes either, but Arjun knows she won't admit it.

'They're divorced, Sunila.'

Sunila sniffs and rubs her nose with the palm of her hand. He knows she is aware that he finds this dismissive gesture disgusting.

He cranes to see whether Sami has bought his ice cream. 'Let him eat his ice cream in here.'

'Not in here. There will be ice cream all over the place.'

'What does it matter?'

'And who has to clean it up?'

There was a time when he would have had more energy over these disputes. He would have found a towel for the boy to sit on while he dripped ice cream happily over himself. But now he has no power, no choice, no freedom to say, 'But it is so' with the finality that comes with a functioning body. The brief memory of energy, of supple strength, is fading.

When the body no longer operates, the self disappears. He feels this diminishing, a gradual receding of who he is, what he likes, how he dresses, where he goes. And he can go nowhere. A short trip to the back window and he is tired enough to have to rest for a while on the sofa before he makes the trip back to the safety of his armchair.

He longs to walk with his grandson by the seashore and go searching for treasure. *Let's dig for gold, Sami.* And he would slyly drop in a few polished pennies so that Sami shouts with delight. If only he could stand and reach up to one of the high shelves for a book that has pictures of elephants. He looks around for Sunila, but she has gone into the kitchen to make tea. Instead, he asks Tarani, 'Can you reach down the elephant book?'

Sami comes bouncing back in with his ice-cream cone with a chocolate flake sticking out proudly, like a small flag. Arjun calls to him, holding the book open. 'Look, Sami, see the tusks? This is a big guy.'

'E'fun?'

'Yes, in India. And the elephants there are as tall as the ceiling.'

Sami's eyes blaze.

'And tigers, too. Huge tigers!'

'Rraarrr!' Sami bounces around the carpet, the ice cream sagging precariously.

'The elephant is bigger than the tiger. And very brave and strong. The tiger won't attack the elephant. The elephant is the real king of the jungle.'

He longs for musculature so that he can hold Sami's hand and give it a gentle squeeze, so that he can open his arms and receive his grandson for a hug, so that Sami can hug him back, or climb him like a tree.

But in the absence of these physical luxuries, he makes his voice as welcoming as possible. He tries to match Sami's enthusiasm with his own weaker echo.

Sami loses interest in being a tiger and wanders around the living room, sucking his cone, the ice cream dripping down over his hand.

Arjun stands carefully, allowing his body to find its balance before leaning forward onto the walker. Slowly, he edges himself to the sofa where he sinks onto a thick cushion.

Sami spins, jumps onto the sofa and thumps against his grandfather.

Arjun is overjoyed to be pummelled by his grandson, even though he feels himself losing his balance. A combination of a fleeting reflex and a wild grab at the walker helps him remain upright.

'Is your ice cream delicious?'

The ice cream is thrust into his face and he opens his mouth to receive the gift. But the muscles don't respond properly. He can't bite and close his mouth around the ice cream, so it smears across his mouth and cheek. He is delighted to taste what Sami can taste. Does he taste more than the cold sweetness, is there a richer chocolate taste in the young mouth?

Sunila comes in and begins fussing. 'All over your face. You're a mess.' She rubs at his face with a paper towel. She puts her sweet, cajoling smile on for Sami. 'Let's go in the garden and you can eat your ice cream there.'

His heart drops. There is nothing he can do. Even if he argues, she will win.

Sami turns to Arjun but Sunila quickly speaks. 'Grandpa's going to stay here while you finish your ice cream. Then you can come in and see him.'

Tarani says, 'Go with Grandma, Sami.'

Sami thrusts out the ice-cream cone again, a last attempt to share, but feminine hands guide him away.

Sunila makes a joke. 'You almost got Grandpa on the nose that time.' She laughs.

He hears them in the kitchen, small exclamations of 'Oh, no' and, 'Oops, let's get you outside quickly' as the women bundle the child into the garden. Sunila goes outside, too, and Tarani, he supposes, is leaning in the doorway. 'Don't get ice cream on the roses, Sami.'

He hears their voices from what sounds like a long way away. If he closes his eyes he will drift away. He is determined not to lose any of Sami's visit, so he levers himself up and inches the walker into the kitchen. At least he can stand by the window and watch.

Sami is walking in slow circles around the lawn, licking around the melting cone. He's eaten the flake. Arjun tries to imagine what it tastes like. His tongue searches his mouth for the memory, but it is gone.

Tarani and Sunila are standing together on the flagstones near the tiny greenhouse. They are probably discussing herbs and how coriander needs this and tomatoes need that. They don't know anything, the pair of them.

Arjun watches his grandson sit on a cement step. He puts his whole mouth over the cone and sucks. Arjun feels uneasy. What if he inhales the ice cream and chokes? He tries to lift his hand to the window to knock, to draw the chattering women's attention.

Sami yanks the ice cream out and drops it on the patio. He looks up at the window at Arjun, his mouth open in astonishment. His face turns red and he screams.

Arjun guesses it's a bee. He waves feebly at the women, but now they are fussing around the child, asking him questions. Sami screams, catching his breath in great swooping sobs.

Arjun finds he is breathing in great gusts, too. What if the boy swallows the sting? Sami will have to go to hospital, be put on a respirator. And what if he is allergic to bee stings?

He tries to knock on the window, but his hand cannot make a fist and his fingers scrape helplessly against the glass. Neither woman looks up; Sami's eyes are squeezed tight. Finally, more by luck than by rational deduction, Tarani manages to open Sami's mouth enough so that she can extract the sting.

He is relieved, his own mouth throbbing in sympathy. The two women manage to bring the boy inside and suddenly the house is filled with his broken heart. An ice cream has bitten him.

The women are trying to console Sami. 'It's only a bee. Nasty thing. It's dead now.'

But Arjun sees that Sami hasn't made the connection between the ice cream and the bee. He has been betrayed and he continues to wail.

Sunila brings a piece of ice. Sami sucks, a strange rattling, noisily incompatible with his weeping.

Arjun pitches his voice so that the boy will hear him. 'Sami, son. The bee was on your ice cream. And when you put the ice cream into your mouth, you put the bee in too. The bee was frightened and so it stung you.'

Sami looks at his grandfather, his breath shaking his body, the piece of ice bulging from one cheek. 'Ah?'

'It stung you. Your mother pulled the sting out. The bee carries a sting in its tail. You bit the bee and it stung you.'

A half-smile wobbles across his face and Arjun wants to lift him into his arms. He nods instead, impatient with the knowledge that his arms won't even stretch out to his grandson.

Tarani gently wipes her son's face and cuddles him. 'There, there, my darling.'

Sunila sits close by. Arjun can see she also wants to do something to take away the pain. At this moment, Arjun loves his wife and daughter with a flaming love that makes his chest hurt.

Sunila says, 'I'll make some iced lemonade. That will make your tongue feel better, Sami.'

Arjun says, 'Don't we have something? Give him medicine.'

Sunila shakes her head and indicates Tarani with her chin. 'He doesn't believe in giving medicine.' *He* meaning Tarani's ex-husband, Hinton, who claims that pain doesn't exist. It's all psychological. Therefore, pain medication is irrelevant. Tarani has told them about the severe period crampings she endured because Hinton insisted she imagined it.

Arjun breathes in to steady himself and speaks quietly. 'Tarani. Hinton is in America. You are here. I don't think Hinton would mind since Sami is in so much pain.'

Tarani, also tearful, looks at Sunila. 'I've got Calpol in my bag. Hinton doesn't know.'

Sunila fetches Tarani's bag and they squeeze a few drops of pink medicine into Sami's mouth.

Tarani whispers into Sami's hair, 'We won't tell him, will we? You're feeling a bit better, aren't you, darling?'

Sami, still shaking with sobs, says, 'Mm, mm.'

Arjun examines Sami's face. There is some swelling around the eyes, but that may be because of the crying. He swallows past the hurtful obstruction in his throat. If only he could open his mouth and take Sami's pain.

Sami is quieter now. Sunila insists on peering into his mouth. Arjun is impatient with her. 'You're poking around there as though you are after a rat.'

'I'm trying to see if he's all right.'

'Take him to the light where you can see better.'

Sunila pushes her finger into Sami's mouth. He begins crying again. She wipes her finger on her apron. 'I think the swelling is going down.'

'No thanks to you.'

The women croon over the crying child again. Arjun hates them and their *hush darling, don't cry, darling.* Poor little Sami.

Finally, Tarani decides it's time to leave. The Calpol appears to be working and Sami has fallen asleep. Arjun clears his throat for the request. 'May I kiss him goodbye?'

There's a barely perceptible signal exchange between Tarani and Sunila. Arjun refuses to let the anger rise up. Tarani lowers the sleeping child so that Arjun can kiss the top of the sleeping child's head. He whispers, 'Be well, son.'

'What was that?' Sunila frowns at him.

Arjun shakes his head. This will be safe from her.

'What did he say?' Sunila asks Tarani but she shrugs.

Arjun says, 'Have a safe journey, pet. Call us when you get home.'

For Sami and Tarani, home is now a flat in Swiss Cottage. Sami likes the roof terrace, where he has started his own garden in a sandbox with petunias named Bolam, Hentiss and Tenklu. Arjun worries about the roof terrace, even though it has a strong, high safety rail. He has cautioned Tarani never to let the boy out of her sight. You never know what growing boys will get up to.

The women's voices trail along the hedge outside as they walk out to the car. He hears Tarani open the car door and imagines her settling Sami in his car seat, buckling him in, nesting his cheek against the cushion. *Goodnight, Sami.*

He listens to the car starting up, the cheerful goodbyes and the engine accelerating away. Silence.

Sunila closes the front door and comes back into the living room. 'Well, time for dinner, I suppose. What do you want to eat?'

'Anything.'

'All right,' she says in her patient voice.

She goes to the kitchen, turns on her Ray Price CD and clatters her pots and pans about. She will be absorbed there for another half an hour.

He clutches his memories greedily to himself. Sami's smile, his hello kiss, open-mouthed, sweet-breathed. His wonder at the elephants. His delight over everything. Arjun wonders, *Was I like that? Ever?*

He feels anger stirring against this ex-husband, this Hinton, who still insists on dictating to Tarani. What idiocy makes a man dismiss pain as though it is some fairy tale? How dare he be so callous? How could Tarani have suffered him for so long?

Memory flings a door off its hinges. Tarani, thirteen, crouched on the floor in tears. They'd been getting ready for a trip to the beach. The car was packed and even Murad, notoriously slow at everything, was dressed and standing in the living room.

And now his daughter was crying. He saw his thirty-four-year-old self, so confident, such authority, hands on hips. 'Leave her, Sunila. She'll soon come round.'

Sunila had murmured to Tarani, 'I'll get you something.'

He had shaken his head. 'No. Don't spoil her.'

Sunila had turned on him. 'She's in *pain*.'

'It's all in her mind.'

He said that?

He hears the rattle of the tray approach, slow and then stop.

Sunila says, 'Arjun?'

But he cannot reply; he weeps, bent over, as though he has dropped his heart somewhere in the folds of the blanket lying crumpled on the floor.

11

THE ABILITY TO WALK
INDEPENDENTLY

MAY 2001

In the old days, Murad would have spent forty minutes in the bathroom, ignoring Arjun banging on the door. Tarani would have been ready to go, but too slow in helping to load the car, or would have brought Arjun the bags in the wrong order. Arré, *this child is so stupid*. Sunila smiles. What a fuss everyone made, but they all had a good time in the end and that's what counts.

Today, though, it's just Arjun and Sunila. These days Arjun no longer has the energy to berate her about being late. He has been ready for some time and is waiting in the living room while she calmly loads the bags in the car. She has a quick shower and dresses. There's even enough time to pin on the little pearl and agate brooch that Pavi gave her a few years ago. How nice to leave in such a civilized manner instead of all that hurry-burry business.

Arjun can no longer drive, so Sunila takes the driver's seat. She dislikes driving on the motorways, but it is Sunday morning with little traffic about and the car settles onto the A40, quickly leaving semi-detached Hayes and Northolt for the tall, narrow houses crammed up against the Westway. The car accelerates up onto the flyover and, for a few moments, they glide past grey and rusty loose-tiled rooftops.

Then they descend back onto the gritty A roads that grind further into London, where the terraces of shops and upstairs flats squat along Seven Sisters Road. Who lives above Mini's Fish and Chips and the Sunshine Market? Do they know each other? What do they do about the smells? Young men jog in baggy trousers and puffy jackets with white stripes along the arms. And everywhere this revolting graffiti disfiguring bridges and walls and even shop windows. Why do young people need to deface everything? Can't they just write their slogans on pieces of paper?

They turn onto Green Lanes. Sunila recognizes more landmarks. 'We're close to Clissold Park, aren't we?'

'Clissold is at the other end.'

'And Lordship Road isn't far away. Remember, in the old days, we used to walk around the cemetery? What was it called?'

'Pay attention, Sunila. We're turning here.'

She turns onto Brownswood Road and into the warren of blocks of flats. Carefully, she manoeuvres the car into a small parking space beside the rubbish skip.

In gradual stages, Arjun levers himself out of the car and up and grasps his walker. She avoids pulling a face but the smells from the skip make her wish that Arjun would hurry up. She loads the pull-along bag with her food bags and they begin the slow walk across to the ground-floor flat that is Pavi and Mike's home. As they get closer to the building, there is the familiar smell of frying bacon along with other smells of garam masala, cumin and onion. Pavi is cooking, but not just Pavi. Sunila glances up. Perhaps there are other Indian families living here now, who also cook like the Kulkanis. Perhaps they slap their chapatti dough on a stone and squat over a small electric hotplate, like Sunila did when she was first in London. It's somehow comforting. They're all in this together, one big block of flats filled with happy families.

Near the front door, someone has spray-painted a small figure with a big stomach and hanging penis, along with the words 'fuck off'.

Arjun says, 'Tchah. Filth. What is the country coming to?'

Before Sunila can reply, the door opens.

'Here's Aunty.'

'Aunty, give us a hug.'

'Suni, Arjun, *bhai*. So lovely to see you. Kids, let your great-uncle through now. Careful.' Pavi shepherds Arjun into the living room.

'Did you bring the pie, Aunty?' Sadiq's head bobs over the confusion of limbs in the hallway.

'I'll pie you in a minute. Let your aunt take her coat off.' Mike shoos the children away.

Sadiq, grown up and prematurely greying, helps Sunila and her plastic bags of curry, rice, dhal and her pie, into the kitchen.

'You *did* bring the pie!' Sadiq unwraps it carefully.

'Of course, Sadiq. I promised, didn't I?' She watches him: this once-upon-a-time imp trained at the Royal College of Music and is now a professional conductor. 'So? Still going to America? Pennsylvania, isn't it?'

'Philadelphia, Aunty. Five nights. Back home for two nights and then off to Glasgow to guest for a month.'

'*What* a busy time you'll have of it. I suppose your wife has something to say about that.' Sunila laughs.

'*She's* all right. It's the *boys*. They complain *all* the time.' He rolls his eyes in a way that brings back the small energetic child who loved to hug her and sit on her lap.

Who would have thought that little Sadiq would grow so tall? So gifted, too, and no airs and graces. Still a fan of her lemon meringue pie.

'My favourite.' He lovingly transfers it to a plate and moves it to the wide windowsill for safety.

He helps to unwrap the rest of the plastic boxes in plastic bags. She watches as he decants the curries into bowls for the microwave. So lovely to see the children growing up and with kids of their own. Then Pavi shoos him out of the kitchen. What is left for Sunila to do?

Sunila has sometimes wondered what it would be like to sit in the living room with the men talking over the old days in India. But what would she have to say about India? And the women in the kitchen were full of *now* and what was happening in the office and what was being worn and who got which promotion (unfairly) and who scandalously slapped the parcel post boy's face. *Young girls these days*, they would shake their heads, *just asking for trouble.*

Even though it was Pavi's kitchen, it was where Sunila used to feel the most comfortable. She'd be elbow to elbow with Mum and the great-aunts, Pavi, Haseena and Nawal, all around the table, sorting lentils, topping and tailing green beans and whipping up butter and sugar for the cake icing. The best jokes were in the kitchen. Sometimes, they would have to stop what they were doing to lean against each other as they laughed.

Now the women have dwindled away. Hard to believe that Nawal, too, is gone. So young, as well. Only sixty-four. Now it's just Sunila, Pavi, Haseena and Great-Aunt Vera, whose ninety-seven years make her the youngest of the great-aunts. Too old to stand around in the kitchen, Great-Aunt Vera is in the living room, dozing in the brown paisley armchair, a light wool blanket over her knees, cup of tea nearby, the last faint wisps of steam disappearing. Great-Aunt Vera is the only one who still takes tea in a cup. Pavi keeps one for her in a cupboard above the sink: flowers around the rim, a gold trim around the saucer and a curly handle that Great-Aunt's arthritic fingers can barely hold.

'How is Tarani? And Sami?' Pavi wipes her hands on her apron. 'Such a sweet little boy.'

'They're visiting America. Hinton, you know, insisting on his father's rights. He's trying to persuade her to move back.'

'Go on – she won't do it, will she?'

'She said to me, she said, "Mum, he was such a bully. Always insulting me, running me down. Never again".'

'Sometimes you don't find out these things until after you're married,' Pavi said.

'And then it's too late.'

They switch places so that Pavi can reach the sink to wash the *kothmir* and Sunila can chop the tomatoes at the table.

'Anyway, she'll be back here with Sami later this year. Tarani is *so* good with Arjun, and how Sami loves his grandfather.' Sunila tips the tomatoes into a bowl.

'Lovely, Suni. And Murad? He's fine, too?'

'Business is growing so fast, nah? Doing very well. No girlfriend yet, though.' Sunila pours dhal into a microwave-proof dish.

'Don't worry, Suni. He'll find someone.'

'I just wish he could settle down. He never tells me anything.'

Pavitra sighs as she lifts down a bowl from one of the cupboards.

'Pavi, are you all right?'

'Fine, fine. Just a little tired.'

'You work too hard.'

Pavi waggles her head. 'So, Suni, we should go out for a good old Chinese chew. There's a new place in Southall. Very cheap. We can make a day of it. I want to find some of those dried chillies, remember the ones we had at Christmas?'

'Let's do it. How about next weekend? Maybe Tarani can come over and sit with Arjun.'

Suddenly the bowl slips from Pavi's hands. Sunila darts forward and snatches it up just before it hits the floor. Pavi looks stunned. 'How did that happen?'

'No harm done.' Sunila puts the bowl back on the table. 'Come, come. Sit. I'll make us a cup of tea.' Sunila offers a kitchen stool and Pavi, who is always the last to sit down during any of the family parties, sinks as though her legs are weighted with cement.

'I don't know what it is, Suni. I've never felt so tired like this.'

'Are you sleeping okay?'

'Sleep is fine.' Pavi looks at the Formica table. 'I've been crying. Stupid of me. I don't have anything to cry about.'

'Has Mike…?'

'No, no. He's been very good, Suni. I couldn't ask for a better…' She looks up at Sunila. 'Well. Anyway.'

Suni swallows the comment she'd like to make about Mike. 'Did someone upset you?' Suni pours the tea and adds milk and sugar the way Pavi likes it. Pavi curls her small hands around the mug.

'You know I'm working part-time, just two days a week, even though I'm officially retired, isn't it? Well, yesterday I had a long report with three copies. I lined up my carbons and sheets of paper as usual and put them into the typewriter. And then I started to cry. Just like that.'

'Were you in pain, Pavi?'

Shakes her head. 'I had to go to the Ladies to pull myself together. I don't know what the others must have thought. It's never happened before.'

Pavi looks so bewildered that Suni puts an arm around her. 'No, darling. All of us have days like that.'

'And do you cry?' Pavi looks up.

'Sometimes. At the bottom of the garden. I pretend I'm putting the compost out.'

The trips to the compost heap are less frequent these days, and anyway, there's no point in dwelling on these things. Just put them behind you. But Pavi is so vulnerable and Sunila feels protective.

'You need a good rest, Pavi.'

The kitchen door opens and Haseena comes in. 'Aunty wants a biscuit to dip in her tea.'

Pavi jumps up but Sunila says, 'You sit there and drink your tea. I'll take care of the biscuits.' She turns to Haseena. 'Chocolate or plain?'

'Rich Tea, if there are any.' Haseena looks at Pavitra. 'Pavi, are you all right?'

'She's fine.' Sunila snaps open the biscuit tin. 'McVitie's.

Will these do? We're just having a cup of tea. Would you like one?'

'Yes, please. I'll take these to Aunty.' Haseena disappears with the tin.

Pavi says, 'It's okay, Suni. I don't mind Haseena knowing. She's family.'

'Of course. It's just that, you know, after that business of her boyfriend—'

'Suni, that was so many years ago. And she didn't know he was married. He kept it a secret from her.'

'Well, she should have known. These men will try anything on.'

'But he told her he was single.'

'How naive could she be? He's an older man. It's obvious he was married. And married men are like that. Always on the prowl.'

'I know.' Haseena has come in quietly.

Sunila jumps. 'I'm sorry, I—'

'It's okay, Suni. I still think about it. Maybe I should have been more suspicious. It *was* silly of me. Nawal told me I should be careful. But…' Haseena stands with the biscuit tin in her hands.

And Sunila sees it. A warm spring morning, the beautiful widow and the handsome man in a pinstriped suit who stops at the shop to admire the lavender sachets, who buys two for his sister. After a couple of weeks, he offers to take Haseena for a cup of coffee. Someone else might have seen it as a typical 'line', but not Haseena, who has never mentioned how lonely she must have been. Sunila pours the tea. All these years she has been unfair to Haseena because Arjun was once attracted to her. Her face becomes warm.

Jesus would have forgiven Haseena, like He forgave the fallen women in the Bible. Not that Haseena is a fallen woman, but she did have two husbands. And what would Jesus have said about Sunila, who has stood on the sidelines, judging? She places a mug of tea in front of Haseena. 'Would you like sugar?'

'That's okay. I don't take sugar.' Haseena looks up. 'Suni?'

And the stupid tears are coming. 'I'm sorry, I'm sorry, Haseena.'

Haseena is on her feet, her arms around Sunila. 'What on earth are you apologizing for?'

'I have thought unkind thoughts about you. I'm ashamed of myself.' Even now it is difficult to put into words.

Haseena is saying 'hush' but Sunila must confess. 'It's not Christ-like, and I must ask you for forgiveness.'

'It's all right, Suni. We're friends, aren't we? I don't know what it is you've done but it's really all right.'

Sunila is a little winded by this sudden generosity. 'Well, it *is* a long time ago now, I suppose.' She smiles a little and wipes her eyes. How easy it is to make things right. She sits at the table with her sisters-in-law. 'Biscuit, anyone?'

It's not meant to be a joke but they all laugh. Perhaps she and Pavi could invite Haseena to join them for the

Chinese lunch. But no. There are some things she wants to keep just for herself and Pavi.

Sadiq wanders in. 'Is it time for lunch, Mum? Aunty?' He addresses whichever aunty happens to look up. 'I can get the kids' plates ready.'

A chorus of *no, no, no, we'll do it.* But as she stands up, Sunila notes the ache in her hip. Pavi is moving more slowly these days, too. And even Haseena, who used to look so young, has grey hair and a double chin. But they stir and serve, quickly making an omelette for the one child who won't eat curry and rice, reaching over and behind each other to lift this bowl and empty that one. The microwave hums and goes off like a pinball machine, and Pavi's best china plates are sent steaming one by one into the dining room at two-minute intervals. In the old days they would have served everyone together and the children would have sat at the kitchen table while the adults sat at the big dining-room table, white tablecloth, white napkins, polished cutlery and plates, water jug, silver salt and pepper pots, steaming bowls all ranged along the centre. This one-by-one business is odd, but at least it's convenient. No hauling endless dishes back and forth along the corridor. Much better, really.

Mum, Nawal, Jonti. How they would have loved to see these nephews and nieces with their children. Just as noisy and happy as it ever was: the shouting, the laughing, a small one crying and being comforted by other small cousins.

Sunila pops her head around the living-room door to check on Arjun and hears the older cousins talking about a visit to some stately home. Their language is a strange mixture, part Cockney. Their vowels concertina, elongate, writhe around and emerge dragged through hedges of consonants that drag or just snap off and disappear.

'It was really lovely, the castle. The architecture and that. But when we got inside, it was a bit of a disappointment.'

'That's what the Christians said about the Colosseum.'

Everyone thinks this is funny, and Sunila retreats before they see her and try to suppress their laughter. She has stopped trying to explain her disapproval of these kinds of jokes, like that one Tarani used to think was so amusing: A *Punch* cartoon of the Christians facing the lions with the caption 'And there was one poor lion that hadn't got a Christian'. Never mind. Never mind. Let them enjoy themselves.

In the kitchen, the microwave is still busily humming. *Has Arjun got enough to eat? Did the children get their chicken? Who needs more chapattis?* Sunila glances over at Pavi. No sign of the earlier anxiety. Firm hands gripping the ladles, the plates, the extra-large rice cooker. When a jar of pickle needs opening, it is Pavi who unscrews the lid.

Sunila admires the easy competence of Sadiq (all grown up) and his cousins who can microwave food, feed their children and sit chatting on the sofas with everyone. It feels as though the centre is no longer in the kitchen with the aunts, but some shifting, nebulous nervous system that depends on where the cousins and their laughter are. Even simple conversation is mined with this difficult computer language that all the youngsters know. Sunila daren't ask any questions in case someone laughs at her. It's better to stay here in the kitchen.

And when everyone else has had seconds and thirds, and the lemon meringue pie, chocolate cake and trifle have vanished and the cousins have washed and dried most of the dishes, Sunila, Pavi and Haseena finally sit down at the kitchen table and serve their own food onto the old plastic melamine plates. They eat in comfortable silence, passing the pickled onions and the Bolst's. And when one lifts the kettle to boil water for tea, another collects the pot from the draining board and spoons in tea leaves, while the third wipes off three mugs and three teaspoons. Sunila's heart is full. This is family.

12

BREATHING ISSUES

JUNE 2002

Arjun sits as close as his wheelchair will permit. His younger sister, Pavitra, slumps in the armchair in front of him. She is sixty-nine. He is seventy-two.

She lives on the fourth floor in an assisted-living building. The flat is small, but with none of the clutter of the previous one where she, her husband, Mike, and the two children jumbled around together – *Where are my socks? Who took my sweater? Are there any bananas left?*

Mike is now in hospital, having suffered his second stroke. Like a musical stop, an unexpected rest, his absence is like a too sudden syncopation; the support for the family's flying melodies has gone. Mike's booming cartoon laugh *hoowaa hoowaa hoowaa* has gone. Mike's tartan tobacco perfuming his embrace has gone. His children wonder at this quiet, empty person who cannot speak but who occasionally squints up at them through his one good eye.

The two sons, both living in Cornwall, shuttle between their father, all hospital smells and rough sheets, and their mother whose memories nestle around the old green and beige history of the London flat. Arjun sees his nephews' shock when Pavitra talks about dying. He sees that Pavitra understands their fear, and he watches her struggle to be a parent despite the confusion, the pain, the overwhelming weariness.

He thinks of the photo albums, their childhood belonging to another land, where they were once without pain: trips to Goa, to the hill stations; smiling groups hugging in front of the Red Fort, on top of stone staircases, and next to sandcastles at the beach. It all belongs to some other once-upon-a-time.

Dying is no longer the repellent bogeyman of younger days. It has become more attractive. Even the word, *dying*, sounds soothing; a gentle sliding away.

The two nephews complain to Arjun about the hospital, the arrogant, cruel nurses, the awful food. They demand better care: they want someone like their parents to take care of their parents.

A tinkling in the kitchen as the day nurse makes tea. The afternoon sun slides down the tall display cabinet. A picture of Pavitra and Mike is angled on the top shelf. Other pictures placed on lower shelves can be seen at a glance, but to see Pavitra and Mike you must sit across the room and look up, almost to the ceiling, as though the photograph is about to disappear to heaven.

Pavitra gasps, 'Why – am – I – so – scared? Why – can't – I – get – any – air – into – my – lungs?'

'Pet, calm down. Try to breathe more slowly. Look, copy me.' He breathes in slowly and pushes out the breath with his mouth open. She tries, but can't copy him since it is unseemly to display her tongue. She breathes in and blows air out, but can't slow down. Her shoulders lift during the intake, the right hitching slightly more than the left, as though trying to help it up. But the air won't go in and nothing she can do will help it.

He wishes to straighten her up, put pillows behind her back and shoulders, settle her so that she will feel more comfortable, relax a little. But he cannot even reach out to hug her.

His left arm no longer functions independently. His right arm can lift the left so that he can scratch the dry skin at his temple. That is as much as the left hand can accomplish. The right arm can push a phone next to his ear, if he can rest the elbow on a table.

He watches his sister's laboured breathing, the blanket dropped around her feet. She has always been a modest woman. He knows she would be embarrassed if she knew her knees were exposed. He cannot reach down to pick up her blanket.

She says, 'They – were – mean – to – me.' She pushes back her right sleeve to show him the deep bruising at her elbow where a syringe was carelessly pushed into the bone. 'That's – why – I – discharged – myself.'

'Pet, don't try to speak.' He knows this story. Perhaps the nurse was bored, irritated, badly paid. Whatever the reason, he is sickened. How could they treat her like this? She is no more than eighty pounds now and her thin arms, lying circled in her lap, look like the last twigs from a ravaged nest.

'Would you like some music?' He looks up at the day nurse but Pavitra shakes her head.

'Please – no – too – loud.'

The day nurse says, 'I don't like all that Britney Spears business. Not like real music, is it?' She puts the tray down and holds out the mug with a straw to Pavitra. 'I'm going down to check with Amy. She said she called the doctor an hour ago. He should have called back by now.' She rustles out of the flat.

Arjun remembers back to when he was a nurse. During one of his night visits to the ward, he found one of the patients having difficulty sleeping. He offered the elderly man a cup of tea. And then another voice whispered, 'Please may I have a cup of tea, too?' He found himself handing round cups of tea while everyone relaxed. Eventually, the word went round and for several days the whole ward sat up at 2 a.m., ready for their tea.

Pavitra's face is thin and her eyes are too large. She looks so little like the photograph at the top of the cabinet. A dark-haired, thirty-year-old Mike, his arm around the tiny woman, leans towards the camera. She sits stiffly, smiling nervously. How old was she? Twenty-two? She looks younger.

Pavitra says, 'Please – call – the – doctor.'

'Pet, calm yourself.'

She still thinks he is capable and he has a moment of triumph and fury. If only it were that simple – to pick up the phone, to make these idiots understand that his sister can't breathe, to force them to come immediately, to bring oxygen, tranquillizers, an old-fashioned kind of nurse who would take charge efficiently. The way he used to.

He must sit in his wheelchair and watch his sister trying to breathe. Is this what is meant by learning patience? He has said nothing when his wife has pulled him from his wheelchair to seat him in the La-Z-Boy, even though it was painful. He has waited while the social worker and the district nurse have discussed him and his failing body as though he is some difficult and fragile problem they must solve. He has eaten what was put in front of him – overcooked vegetables and small squares of toast with Marmite – even though he hates Marmite and longs for brisket cooked in red wine. He has sat in the shower, naked in front of his wife, who helps him to wash, bowing his head as he waits for the water to fall.

And is it impatient to wish to stand up, walk to the phone, pick it up, dial the number and use a strong voice to summon help? *Precious Lord, take my hand. Lead me on, let me stand.* His god, tentatively standing on the other side of the living room, doesn't make eye contact. Arjun is enraged. *What good are you?* His god touches the photo frames, looks into the pictures, examines the skirting board. Even a look of understanding would help, some small gesture to show Arjun that he isn't alone. He wonders if this god is sent to mock him, standing just out of reach, ignoring pain and focusing on trivia.

Pavitra says, 'These – nurses – are – Africans.'

He says, 'They don't mean you any harm. They are used to poor treatment in their own country. So they can't understand how to treat people gently. They aren't like American nurses.'

She nods, accepting the excuse. Whoever they are, Africans, British, Indians, Californians, he hates them for despising and mistreating the old.

She says, 'If – it – was – a – young – person – they – would – try – harder.'

He agrees.

She is too weak to cry. He tries to talk about the children, the grandchildren, but his voice is soft and she is deaf. Her blue hearing aid hangs off her right ear like some strange Christmas-tree ornament. He doesn't know if the battery is working.

He talks on. At first, she bends her head towards him, then leans back, her shoulders still moving up and down under her internal seismic shifting. Something in his voice must reach her and she closes her eyes. His throat becomes tight as she finally sleeps. He talks on.

The time he climbed a tree and she wanted to follow him up. How old was she? Seven? He must have been ten or eleven. He eventually climbed down and pushed her up, his shoulder under her bony bottom. She scrambled, small hands unable to find a handhold. 'This tree's too hard for me.' But he continued to heave and she finally made it to the lowest branch, about eight feet above the ground. He climbed above her but she remained where she was, content to sit in the fork and look out over the meadow to the foothills of the Himalayas.

He climbed down and left her in the tree. She called after him, but he shook his head as he walked away. 'You can climb down yourself.' She was angry. 'I don't care. I want to stay in this tree anyway.' He went far enough to be sure she couldn't see him through the trees, and then wormed back through the tall grass to see what she would do.

For a while she sat staring in the direction he'd gone. He knew what she was thinking. *He'll come back.* And then she started to cry. He almost ran to her, but then she began to extend one foot, searching for a hold on the tree trunk.

She released the upper branch and hugged the lower branch with both arms, easing herself down. Her legs dangled and kicked. He knew she'd be sobbing, but she was a determined little thing. Look how she'd followed him up.

Finally, one foot connected with a large knot on the tree trunk and she stabilized, transferring her weight so she could move her body further down. She bent, placing one hand down on the knot.

As she lowered her body to the ground he saw her chest heaving with the effort. She stood up and brushed off her dress, examined her knees and then shook her hair back. How proud she looked. How proud he was.

His voice is almost gone. Amy arrives. 'The bus is here to take you home, Mr Kulkani. And the doctor is on his way to see Pavitra.'

He says, 'Don't wake her.' He watches her sleeping face, the lined cheeks sagging. But in the afternoon light, he imagines she looks a little like his tree-climbing sister.

His god, the shuffling bumbler, is turning to leave but, Arjun is almost sure, there is a faint smile.

He will not see Pavi again. Once the doctor finally comes, they'll take her back to the hospital.

As they wheel him out to the lift, he wonders if she is dreaming of climbing up into the branches of the tallest tree in Mussoorie. She can see so far; she can see their school, their house and away to the snow-capped peaks of the Himalayas and to the white sky beyond.

It has been their custom to pray after his visits. He prays to his shuffling god, imbues him with more power for this task. *Lord, please hold my sister. Bring her peace. Keep her in Your hand and give her the rest she so needs.*

He bows his head as the lift descends to the ground floor. *Lord. Oh, Lord. Please let her die.*

13

REDUCED DEEP-TENDON REFLEXES

JULY 2003

Six a.m. From the kitchen window, Sunila can see that the wood pigeons have knocked over their water dish again, the silly things. She opens the back door and steps out into the cool morning air. She refills the water dish from the hose and places a large stone in the middle to weigh it down. She glances up at the rose bushes. All these dead heads. A few minutes will take care of them. The secateurs are hanging on a nail inside the shed door. She puts on her gloves and collects the compost bag, breathes in the sleepy, damp, morning earth smell, the milk-blue sky promising another hot one. She snips at the withered flowers and drops them into the bag. One of the deep yellow roses has opened to reveal faint pink streaks on its inner petals. She inhales the scent and closes her eyes. A beautiful English country garden. *You are nearer God's heart in a garden than anywhere else on earth.*

She brushes her hair back with her wrist. The wood pigeons haven't come back yet. The first sun is warming a small orange and black butterfly on one of the lobelia bushes. What's that song about the butterfly? 'I chase the la-la-la-la butterfly of love.' Such a pretty melody.

The butterfly stutters away along the fence and over a patch of bright colour. Between the pots at the bottom of the garden is a young fox, lying there, as bold as you please, soaking up the sun. He's probably already done his business on the lavender. Dirty beast. His coat catches the light and his tail lies across the earth like the long, fluffy brush she uses for dusting around the picture frames. His quick breath moves his body up and down. He looks like a drawing from a children's book: white whiskers, amber eyes, slender black forepaws like a dancer's feet. He stands up, widens his rear legs, and she realizes he is going to do more business right there.

'Not on my lobelias, you don't!' She raises the secateurs and rushes at him. His head pops up like a flag and he is a red streak through the fence. She bends down to look through the narrow gap, half expecting to see his mocking narrow face. Nothing but dense green bush. He might be in the middle, laughing at her, or he might be several gardens away.

'And stay out.' She marches back to the shed to deposit her secateurs and gloves. She empties her bag into the compost heap. Cheeky bounder. She'll have to block that gap in the fence.

She steps inside the kitchen to collect her tea and then sit on the back step. Despite the fox, the morning is still perfect and she can relax for a moment to inhale the drifting scents from the flowers. That peony needs repotting. Perhaps she can do it later after she's attended to Arjun.

'Sunila?'

She sighs. A few moments of peace and quiet. Is it too much to ask?

'Sunila?' Seventy-five and he still has such a loud voice.

'I'm coming.' The words sound irritable. She tries a brighter note. 'Just closing the back door.' But the door slips out of her fingers and slams shut. She puts her tea down on the counter. No chance of drinking that now. She hurries into the living room. Arjun is standing up and leaning on the walker.

'Good morning, Arjun. How are you?'

The body is less. The legs are another pair of folds in his pyjama trousers. The hands, long thin fingers that used to carve descriptions, edicts, stories, out of the air, are now speechless in his lap. He used to be able to type emails to friends in India. Now he has to use both hands to grasp a pencil, the rubber tip-tapping out messages, key by key. The thin hair no longer disguises the dark marks of age spreading maps across his skull and cheek. His skin, always dry, has developed spots that turn into red welts that peel and weep if they are not regularly rubbed with cream.

The back of his head is always itchy, his ankles, his knees, his elbows and wrists.

'Please open the door.' He pushes the walker.

She can see it; the stumble, the fall, the crack of bone. 'Don't go so quickly. I'm coming.'

'Don't fuss, Sunila.'

'You're so impatient. You'll break your hip and then where will we be?'

'I'm not going to break my hip.'

She opens the door wide and stands back.

He moves slowly, finding the rhythm of walking. She watches him as he navigates the doorway and trundles through to the toilet.

'Thank you.' His voice comes back with a slight echo. It's only the bathroom acoustics but it sounds as though he's calling from another world. She shivers, goes back into the kitchen.

She considers turning on her cassette player but decides to wait until he's finished. How much longer before he is unable to shave or wash, to comb his hair? These days she has to help him pull his trousers on. She finds a pullover, tracksuit bottoms, socks and the comfortable boxer shorts he now prefers. The small pile of clothes is so much smaller.

Was it so long ago when he used to wear a shirt and tie and a suit for work? He'd stand in front of the mirror, deftly knotting his tie in a half-Windsor. How proud she was to see him take his place on the rostrum in church, right next to the pastor and senior elder. Humble and all, but so nicely dressed. She remembers the ceremony to ordain him. She'd sat in a pew towards the back of the church, covertly watching the other church members seeing her Arjun elevated to this important position: an Indian and no different from any of them.

These days they don't go to church. It's too much for Arjun, who has to sit near the back in case he needs the toilet. And she won't go alone. All that pity. And they call themselves Christians. They're gloating over the fact that the Kulkanis no longer hold so much influence in the church. *How the mighty have fallen.* Well. God knows what's in people's hearts and they'll get what's coming on Judgement Day.

The phone rings. Arjun calls out from the bathroom. 'Get the phone.'

'I know. I heard it.' She hurries to pick up the receiver.

'Mum!'

She sits down suddenly on the sofa where Arjun's sheets and blankets are still muddled together.

'Murad?' Her voice dries up.

'How *are* you? Sorry I haven't called for a while. It's been crazy at the shop.'

'Oh, Murad!' She feels herself pouring into his name. Three months since they last spoke, and then only briefly because he was leaving *on safari.*

'So, how's everything? Dad holding up?' *Dead.* 1974 when he first moved to Australia and only a year later when he became this new, bouncy voice on the phone. He's forty-nine now and the years have settled the stretch into his voice.

'He's fine. He's just in the bathroom having his wash. I'll call him.'

'In a minute. Tell me about yourself first?' He sounds so *perky*.

'Well, I, I don't know. I went to Sainsbury's yesterday?' Without realizing it, Sunila copies the question-like style of their conversation.

'Sainsbury's? Still there, then?' Murad chuckles. 'Good old Sainsbury's. Marks and Sparks too, I bet? You like your Marks and Sparks.'

'Ye-es.' Sunila is hesitant. Is Murad making fun of Marks and Spencer?

'Can't remember the last time I went there. Must be—'

'Five years. Since you were here.'

'Five years? That long? I can't believe it. So, Mum, still doing your hospital work?'

'That's changed now. The hospital work takes almost all day. I can't leave your father—'

'That's right. Of course you can't go.' Murad's voice is softer. 'You probably don't get out much at all, do you?'

'Well, I do the shopping. At good old Sainsbury's.' She laughs a little and Murad laughs too. 'And the post office. You know, here and there. Short trips. Sometimes I go on the bus to Uxbridge. It's a new line. It's just around the corner on Adelphi Crescent.'

'The U7, isn't it? Goes along Charville and up Pole Hill. Took it into Uxbridge last time I came over.' He sounds more like his old self.

'That's right. Your old school.'

'Mellow Lane. I used to bike to school up Pole Hill.' *Mella Line. Oi used to boike.*

'I remember when you came home and told me. "Mum, I made it up Pole Hill."'

Murad laughs. 'Quite a climb, eh? The rolling hills of Hayes.' *Heels of Highs.*

'No hills here, son. All flat as far as the eye can see.'

'I know. A lot of flat bits out here, too. But not where I am. And you should see the rainforest, Mum. We do four or five tours a week now.'

The name of his company comes back just in time. 'What happened to the Ride the Bay, the kayaking and all?'

'We're doing a fair bit of business so we've expanded into these eco-rainforest tours. People are wild for eco-anything.' His voice is unstretching a bit; more like his younger self. 'But Mum, it's beautiful. The flowers. Amazing.'

Murad describes the Bumpy Satin Ash, the Red-Fruited Palm Lily and the nectar of the Golden Penda that attracts parrots. He never showed any interest in gardening when he was living here. Why couldn't he have loved her garden?

'Yes, I do like flowers,' she says weakly. Even her Papa Meilland rose, with its deep red velvet petals and throaty scent, can't compete with some big, gaudy, yellow thing that parrots prefer. 'Murad, you know I'd love to come and see your rainforest, but, you know, your father's flying days are over.'

The words fall into some kind of air duct between London and Queensland. Do they boom and echo on their way to the wide Australian deserts where Kipling's Old Man Kangaroo hops through the saltpans, whatever saltpans are? These days her phone conversations with Murad are hinged on fence posts that become further and further apart. It's as though a time machine has whisked Murad into some other galaxy and she can only watch through a small, misty porthole.

How wonderful it would be to travel again: the anticipation of leaving, feeling the ground drop as the plane lifts up, pushing through the clouds to another world where there is always sunshine. Dorothy Frances Gurney might have felt nearer to God's heart in a garden, but Sunila has always felt closest to God in an aeroplane. How liberating it is to fly. No one asks you for anything, no one complains if the food isn't hot enough, no one asks if you've potted the begonias.

'Ah, Mum, I was only joking. Can you imagine getting Dad on a plane? I'm coming over to see you. Three weeks' time.'

'Really? Murad, are you really coming?' She runs out to bang on the bathroom door. 'Arjun! Murad is coming!' She turns back to the phone and ignores the muted roar of protest from the bathroom. 'This is the best news I've heard in a long time. It will be so lovely to have you here. You can have your old room. I'll have to clear a few things away.'

'Actually, I thought I'd stay at a bed and breakfast—'

'What are you talking bed-and-breakfast nonsense? Why spend all that money? I just have to move some of Dad's stuff out of the way.' She hesitates. 'We've redecorated it since you last saw it. Dad's favourite colour. Pink.'

Murad clears his throat. 'Listen, Mum, you don't have to—'

Murad, here. After five years. 'Now. Tell me what you'd like to eat. I usually cook curry and rice for Dad.'

'Anything, Mum. Curry is fine. We don't have a lot of Indian restaurants around here. Mind you, there's a Thai-Indian fusion place. Bombay prawns. Pakoras. *Amritsari* fish. Amazing.'

'Darling, as you know, we – we don't eat prawns. And we don't have deep-fried food. It's not good for your father.'

'Oh, no worries, Mum. Whatever you cook will be fine. So, let me give you the flight times—'

But her heart is bursting for her son. 'Murad. If you want prawns, I'll get for you.'

'No, don't do that, Mum. I know you're not allowed to eat seafood.'

Bottom feeders, the Seventh-day Adventists call them. But wouldn't Jesus get prawns for His son if he wanted them? Is it blasphemous to think of Jesus having a son?

'The flight's coming in at some terrible hour. It's Air New Zealand. Do you have a pen?'

She finds a pen in the kitchen and shakily writes down the details. She hears Arjun trundling back into the living room. She follows him to his armchair and holds out the phone as he takes forever to turn around, position himself at the edge of the chair, lower himself onto the seat, push the walker out of the way, retrieve his handkerchief and blow his nose, tuck the handkerchief back into his pocket and finally sit back and take the phone. 'Hello, son? You're coming to see us?'

Murad is coming. Murad is going to be right in front of her, eating her food, drinking her mango lassi and telling her all his news; Murad who always understood her much more than any close friend. When Murad sees her he will understand, without explanation, how she has had to care for Arjun day and night. He'll see how she has anticipated and answered all of Arjun's demands. He will understand all her lost hours, her wasted days, the self-denial that has reduced her shopping trips to once a week. He will wipe away her tears and there will be no more suffering.

She carefully copies Murad's flight times on the calendar. Two whole weeks. He can't stay longer, of course, because of his business. Demanding and all, but look at what it has done for him: so strong and independent, even if he does talk a bit funny. How wonderful it would be to tell everyone at church. They'd be happy for him, too, so it wouldn't count as boasting. Perhaps Arjun might consider going to the Harrow church next Saturday, just for the second service. She glances at him, cradling the phone in both hands, the fingers unable to grasp.

'So, how's Australia, then?'

Will Murad tell Arjun about the flowers in the rainforest? What secrets can she hold on to, that Murad will tell her not to tell anyone? She remembers the long-ago days of whispering in the kitchen when Arjun was in the next room or upstairs: *don't tell Dad...*

Arjun doesn't talk to Murad for long. His arms are tired and he hands the receiver back with, 'See you soon, son.' She grabs at the phone.

'I won't keep you long. I just wanted to ask if you would eat kedgeree—'

'Mum, I've met someone.'

'A girl?'

'No, a boy. Just kidding.' Murad laughs. 'She's got her own business. Scuba-diving.'

'My goodness, well, that *is* good news. I'm so happy for you. Owns her own business, too, just like you. How lovely.'

'And she's coming with me. To England. That's why we'll probably stay at a B&B. It'd be a bit of a squash in the pink room upstairs.'

'A B&B?' Sunila can't keep the surprise out of her voice. Murad is forty-nine and yet she is embarrassed about him discussing his sleeping arrangements. 'I suppose that might be best.'

'No worries. Really. Sasha's pretty easygoing, anyway.'

'Sasha? Very nice. Is she, ah, Indian?'

'Indian? No. She's a born-and-bred Aussie.'

Aussie. Relief. Not Indian and not one of those Aborigines. Of course, there's nothing wrong with Indians or Aborigines. Some of them can be very nice.

'So where did you meet her?'

'Travel adventure convention. Our stalls were right opposite each other. Ride the Bay and CoolDive. Loads of people around her stall, too.'

'That sounds nice. How old is she?'

'Forty-one.'

Eight years younger than Murad. The fading dreams of grandchildren crack, fragment and pixel away. Even Tarani's pregnancy was touch and go. Still, an active forty-one-year-old might have a chance.

'Isn't she a bit old to go scuba-diving?' Beat. 'It's not that she's *too* old. Forty-one is young, isn't it? It just seems strenuous, that heavy equipment and being in the water all day.'

'It's all right, Mum. Sasha's been scuba-diving all her life. And you should see her. She's got so much energy.'

Sunila imagines her grey-haired son with his pot belly and a slightly less grey-haired, pot-bellied woman standing on the bottom of the ocean floor in their diving gear. She's seen these sporty older women with their overbaked skin. Is this Sasha a hearty type? Does she say 'G'day'?

'And how long have you known each other?'

'Let's see. Must be a year now.'

He talks on about Sasha while Sunila bites back the words. *And it took until now to tell me?* Murad has always been cautious. He just wanted to be sure about Sasha. And it's a good thing that he's waited before bringing someone all the way to England for a visit. Should she ask about Sasha's parents, or will Murad take offence? But he is saying goodbye and there's no time to ask more questions.

The reality hits her. She won't have Murad to herself. No late-night chats over tea and biscuits. No opportunities to talk to Murad about God's plan for him. Even though it's been thirty years since Murad left the church, she still talks to him about Jesus. It's her responsibility. She would like to remind him of *Honour thy father and thy mother*. There's no honouring involved with sons who uproot and tear off to Australia.

It's all very well owning a business. Nice to say to the friends and neighbours, *Oh Murad's business is flourishing. Cairns, you know.* But this kayaking; what is the attraction of straining your arms and back? By all means, go to the seaside. Jesus loved Galilee, although she can't imagine Him paddling about in a yellow plastic boat. And what is wrong with having a business in England? So many nice places to kayak, like Brighton or Cornwall. And then there's the Lake District.

And how will Arjun take the news that some scuba-diving stranger is coming with Murad? The truth is that Arjun may not have much longer. His trips to the toilet are much slower. His voice is weaker. He sleeps less at nights, nods off during the day. But how happy Arjun will be to see Murad. The last time, Arjun stayed awake for nearly all of Murad's descriptions of Cairns and the funny kayaking stories. She can see that Arjun is as baffled as she is over Murad's choice of business, but at least Murad is happy. That's what counts.

Murad *should* be happy; he should have a partner. What is life unless you have someone to talk to? She will tell him that when she sees him, and he will smile at her in his gentle way. *Yes, Mum.* The thought makes her want to cook or clean something. That kitchen windowsill could use a good wipe down. She rinses the cloth out under the cold tap. But she cannot fight back the feeling that she has lost some small, comforting thing that once shaped the whole day. She stops mid-scrub. She will never get it back.

14

WEAKNESS OF THE FACIAL AND TONGUE MUSCLES

PHONE CALL:

Sami: I can't sleep.
Arjun: You're having a hard time, aren't you?
Sami: I'm very boring at night. There's no sleep anywhere.

To: taranikulkani@gmail.com

Dear Sami,

Sometimes I think that rain washes sleep away and that is why you could not find any. I'll bet tonight you'll find quite a bit of sleep and it will be all washed and fresh from the rain.

All last night and this morning we had some snow but mostly

wind. When this happened, I couldn't find any sleep either but it didn't wash away with rain. It got so cold that the sleep turned to ice and froze like an ice cube. Now that the sun is out, I hope that it melts enough sleep so I can find it tonight, just like you will!

Love

Grandpa

AUGUST 2004

A life measured in buttons. Arjun presses the button that elevates him into a sitting position on his bed. If he waits a moment he will have sufficient energy to ease himself sideways into the wheelchair next to the bed. But the energy doesn't come. There's no more mystery about where the energy went. Energy doesn't come to the elderly, or to those whose diseases are taking them, piece by piece. The firing of neurons is now a faint kindling.

Once those fires used to take him, without conscious thought, to church where he stood beside the pastor. He remembers, once, how he lightly ran down the steps from the rostrum to help old Mrs Baldwin stand up to read from the Bible. How fragile her shoulders were under the blue polka-dotted jacket, and the thin hands that shook inside the white gloves. How grateful she was, smiling at him from beneath the brim of the white hat, as he steadied her after her reading and helped her back to her seat. She must have been terrified, wondering if her legs would give way, if she would lose her balance. What courage she had; something he can understand now.

Jonti, once compact, body thin and helpless and shaking, Nawal gently buttoning his shirt. 'See what I have to put up with, *bhai*? Treated like a baby, only. And this Nawal.' A quivering hand dancing in the air, reaching to touch Nawal's cheek. 'How she takes advantage, isn't it? Signs the girls up for some fancy summer camp in Bournemouth. She says I wobbled my head yes. But she knows I can't wobble my head no.' And Nawal holding the quivering palm against her cheek. His eyes on hers, the only focus his body can manage.

Once it was easy to rock up, to use his body's weight to ease himself off the mattress. He actually used to walk to the bathroom. But he has learned to wait. Most of the body's cravings can be subdued, as he learned even before he became sick.

The miracle that he once had a lean, muscular body. Some of the women from the club used to pass comments and smile when he played in squash tournaments. Could he have had coffee with one of them, or even an affair? What was he like, back then, that these ridiculous ideas were feasible?

Back then he was a young, healthy thirty-six. He wore white shorts and ran after small rubber balls with speed and accuracy. Surely he was a superman in those days. Do those other squash players from *back then* also lie in bed wondering where their bodies went, wondering at what date the synaptic rush and response slowed and failed?

Further back was his boyhood in India. How easily, fluidly, he ran up and down mountains as though up were almost the same as down. How he jumped over rocks, between rocks, balancing with his arms flung out, his body leaning this way and that as the impetus carried him forward, forward.

In some faint responsive memory of movement, he moves his legs and finds he can edge himself gradually, carefully, into the wheelchair without catching his feet on the coverlet. He smiles at the triumph; he can still get out of bed by himself, which means he can still go to the toilet by himself. Small victories. He can't even boast to Sami, who is not only well past the stage of getting out of bed by himself but doesn't need a safety rail at night any more.

Arjun realizes, with humility, that he is far behind his grandson, now bounding ahead into his future. At one time he was angry: if the brain could regenerate cells, why couldn't his body rebuild muscles so that he could walk in the garden with his grandson?

He has become accustomed to letting go. He is no longer anxious to keep up with Sami whose world no longer contains Arjun's stories of tigers and elephants, or descriptions of the Himalayas, the old peanut and monkey jokes. Sami writes his own stories now and Tarani types them in emails to Arjun:

Et all your los
Eat all your lunch

Et samwis et noodlos ed pasdo
Eat sandwiches, eat noodles, eat pasta

I like pars a lot
I like pears a lot

Occasional accounts about his grandchild's progress in pre-school are enough. Arjun is content to love from a distance.

More buttons: one to release the brake, one to start the chair rolling forward, and a small handle to direct the chair through the doorway. He remembers to tear off some sheets of paper before he uses the horizontal bar to help lift himself onto the seat.

How long has it been since he was indignant about having to sit to urinate? Now he is merely relieved to sit instead of having to stand.

What importance he used to attribute to small things: his perfectly ironed shirts, the knife-like crease in his trousers, the well-tailored jackets and suits, his meticulously folded socks and underwear, his Kiwi-polished shoes, his leather wallet. These details made him feel a little taller, a little better prepared to face the hostile country he had moved to.

It was Tarani's job to lay the table, but she never did it properly. He remembers that he would make Tarani straighten knives, move glasses over an inch or two so they were correctly aligned, refold the napkins properly. A well-laid table brought a kind of grace to the meal.

Murad's job was to wash the dishes while Tarani dried. Murad was methodical. Tarani was careless, swiping at plates and rubbing handfuls of cutlery together in the towel and jumbling them into the drawer. How many times did Arjun have to order her back into the kitchen where she angrily redried plates and pans, or disentangled the spoons and forks and knives, throwing them into their dividers?

It all meant something, some sense of striving for decorum and order, some sense of fitting in to the middle-class neighbourhood whose ideals he's never quite grasped.

But their neighbours are now used to them. They've been there for fifty years; they're the old-timers. He's seen nearly all the houses on the street change owners at one time or another.

Now they are the sweet old couple at number four, Oriole Drive (*ah, bless*). Sunila greets everyone with a friendly smile and wave, invites them in for tea, hands out biscuits to the children on their way home from school. She has achieved her coveted position of being accepted. She is harmless and old.

Her high heels no longer strike static from the pavement as she busies to work and back home again with carrier bags of groceries. The children are gone; there is no one to scream at in the evenings. She can't even scold him for long without becoming breathless.

He used to laugh at her as she retreated to the kitchen coughing and angry. But now he sees that this is how she stays alive. This is the vigour that allows her to dress him, cook for him, wash him, help him to the bathroom in the day, turn the TV on or off, fetch his photograph albums, take them away when they are too heavy to hold, fetch down books for him and reshelve them when he can't remember the page he wants.

Now he becomes anxious if she coughs too much. He urges her to rest, to take more time watching her soap operas on her bedroom TV. Like him, she also can no longer tolerate the news. What has happened to 'England's green and pleasant land'? It is so far outside his and Sunila's comprehension that it's best to shut it all out. They enquire after each other's health almost tenderly. Did she sleep? How many hours? Was he restless? Did he have to get up more than twice in the night?

Another button to flush and he transfers himself back into the wheelchair, finds his way back without bumping into the door. As he shifts gingerly from wheelchair to bed, he has the impression that someone else is in the room. Perhaps Sunila heard the toilet flush and came downstairs.

He leans back against the elevated bed, catches his breath and says, 'Did I wake you?'

'You might have done, you took that long, you stupid old git.' The voice is young, male and cold. A flashlight is shone directly at his face. There is a crash and swearing as the flashlight is dropped and a chair is overturned. He expects a blow to the head; he must die now. He hopes he will have enough breath to say that they have very little money in the house, but to take whatever there is down here. There is nothing upstairs. Perhaps he can save Sunila from this final shame of being humiliated and hurt by a maniac child.

But the blow doesn't arrive. There is heavy breathing and the voice says, 'You're Indian, intcha?'

Arjun manages, 'Take what we have. I'll tell you where it is.'

'I can't take nothing from you, you old *bhenchod*.'

Arjun flinches at the language. Even now he cannot accustom himself to the casual way that young people swear. And then he realizes the boy is Indian, hence the swearing in Hindi.

'*Beta*, don't hurt us.'

'Shut up. Don't say anything.' A pause. '*Madarchod*.'

'*Beta*, please don't swear.'

'Don't call me son. I'm not your son.'

Arjun tries to slow his breathing down before the panic attack starts. The words are coming with difficulty but at least he can deliver short sentences. If he has to explain anything, he is done for.

'What the fuck am I meant to do now? I mean, I come all this way to break into your *bhenchod* house and you're fucking *Indian*.'

'Son, could you put the light on?'

'Oh yes. Rub it in. Not only can I not smash your *madarchod* head in and take your money, I have to turn the light on so you can make a positive ID for the police. Well, why not? Why fucking not?' There is patting and slapping as the young boy feels his way around the room. More swearing as he contacts the sharp edges of the cupboard. Then the light is turned on. Arjun doesn't move.

The intruder comes around to him. He is a large boy dressed in a black tracksuit and a black balaclava that obscures his nose and mouth. The holes for the eyes are large and Arjun can see that he has thick eyebrows that are bunched together in anger or, perhaps, anxiety.

As Arjun blinks against the light, the boy's eyes come into focus. 'So young.'

Slightly muffled by the wool, the boy says, 'You don't know how old I am, do ya?'

Arjun considers. 'Sixteen? Seventeen?'

'You're wrong. I'm fifteen.'

'*Such* a big boy.'

'My mum's side. We're all big. You should see my sister. She's huge.'

Arjun has a vivid picture of a teenage girl crammed into a tracksuit wearing a similar balaclava and tries to dismiss it before he starts smiling. This is no smiling matter.

Despite the fact that the child is so young, he could easily do a lot of damage. He takes a careful breath.

'I'll tell you where the money is.'

A sigh. 'Nah. I can't take your money, Uncle.'

'But you went to all this trouble.' He breathes in and out. 'Breaking in and what-all.'

'How come you're Indian? Me mates said no one's Indian over on this side.'

Behind the balaclava, Arjun thinks there may be a ferocious sulk going on.

'No other Indian families moved in this side. What to do?'

'How long you been here, then?'

'Almost fifty years.' Breath. 'We've seen so many people leave and new ones arrive.'

'Yeah, well, I didn't come here to listen to all that.'

'Son, that cupboard over there.' Breath. 'There's money. Take.'

The boy pulls the cupboard door open, squats down and pulls out a few envelopes. He leaves them on the floor. 'If only I'd hit you like I was planning. Then I could've taken the money and run.' He pushes at the balaclava. 'It's like Samar says. I'm rubbish at this.'

'But if you'd hit me first,' breath, 'I couldn't tell you about the money.'

'Yeah, but I *hit* you until you *tell* me.'

Arjun imagines the boy sitting enthralled in front of a TV show. 'Son, that hitting is for stronger fellows.' Breath. 'One hit, *pachaak*, and I'm gone.'

'Yeah. You can't even breathe properly. You're really old, innit. No offence, like.'

'Seventy-five.'

'Fuck me. Sorry, Uncle.' The boy sighs. 'I better go.' *Ah be'uh go.* The glottal stop swallows the words, turning them into some peculiar dialect. The young have no patience with language.

Arjun is curious. 'How did you get in?'

'Your front door, mate. You want to change the locks.'

Alert to the noises of the house, he hears Sunila moving upstairs. 'Son, go quickly. My wife is upstairs.' Breath. 'She has the red emergency button.'

'Shit. I'm off. Listen, Uncle, get a deadbolt.' He hesitates, snatches up one of the envelopes and exits through the front door, slamming it behind him.

Arjun listens for the running feet, but there is nothing. Despite his bulk, the boy is light on his feet. He admires the ingenuity. He must be experienced at breaking in to deal with their lock so easily.

'Sunila. Come down. He has gone.' His voice is so weak he is certain she can't have heard.

'Arjun? Are you all right?' Her voice is shaking.

'I'm fine.' His heart rate is returning to normal but he cannot project enough force into his voice to send it up to her.

'Are you there?'

'Yes, I'm here.' He is frustrated with this upstairs-downstairs business. Must they shout for the whole neighbourhood to hear?

'Has the robber gone?'

'He's gone, you deaf old cow.' He is shocked into coughing at his bad language, but there is a small pleasure in the fact that she can't hear him.

'I called the police.'

The flashing blue lights reflect through the curtains and he knows he will not tell the police that the thief was just a child.

The police enter, check the premises, ask him questions that he is now almost too tired to answer. No, he didn't hear the thief enter. No, he didn't get a look at the thief's face. No, the thief didn't talk much to him, other than make vague threats. No, the thief didn't harm him.

'You're lucky, sir. You could have been badly injured. It's mainly kids. They're after drug money. You know how it is.' Arjun doesn't know how it is, but he nods anyway.

Sunila is brought downstairs. She can barely walk and when she sees him, she clings to the policewoman and weeps. 'Arjun… Arjun.'

He suddenly realizes she thought he was dead and was terrified of having to see his body. She continued to call to him because she didn't want to believe he wasn't dead. He imagines her crouched beneath the windowsill, believing she was finally alone.

Her eyes are puffy from crying and she is leaning against the policewoman. He has a moment of sympathy for the officer. Sunila is not a lightweight.

Another policewoman is patting her shoulder. 'Mrs Kulkani, everything is all right. Your husband is fine.'

But she weeps noisily. 'I thought he was dead! I thought he'd been killed!'

Really. There is something indelicate, this shouting about his death with such gusto.

One of the officers speaks to him. 'Mr Kulkani, I'm sorry to take up so much of your time. You must be very tired. I wonder if we could send someone over to talk to you tomorrow?'

'Yes. That's fine.'

The officer collects the others, but not before someone has brought Sunila a cup of tea. The tea-bearing policewoman looks over at Arjun. 'Can I get you one?'

'No, thank you.'

Sunila stands up, in charge again. 'He must get his rest. He's not well, you know.' The officers pat her as though she is a well-behaved dog. She smiles up at them and sees them to the door.

'Arjun, are you all right?'

'I'm tired, Sunila. I want to sleep.'

'But we must talk about it, isn't it? Did you see the robber? What was he like? I heard all the banging and thumping. I crept to the top of the stairs and saw the light go on and someone in black moving around. I thought he was beating you.' Is there a kind of relish in her voice? 'Did he steal anything?'

'He wanted money.'

She sees the open cabinet door. 'He took our money?'

'Not all. Just one envelope.'

'But that was for the poor people in Chad. I was going to send it to the mission. And now it's gone. What am I going to tell them? They'll think I just spent the money on myself.'

'Sunila, no one will think that.'

She is sorting through her envelopes and stacking them neatly back in the cabinet. How often he has told her not to leave money there, but she won't listen.

'Of course, he would take the one with the most money. They're like that, you know. And now those poor people in Chad will have to do without.'

She closes the cabinet door and stands up. 'Well, that's it. Nothing to be done. No good crying over spilt milk. Are you hungry?'

I'm not hungry: I am exhausted from nearly being killed by a foolish child. How can you stand there babbling about money for Chad?

And then he realizes: he is hungry.

'I've got some of that chicken curry. We can have with pilau, yes?'

She bustles off to heat the food and he feels the anger subsiding. The comfortable noises of plates and silverware, the *thunk* and *ka-thunk* of the microwave door opening and shutting. The hum as it starts heating the food. The water from the tap streams into the sink and she fills the kettle for tea. The fridge is opened and he hears the *tuk* of Tupperware being opened. She must have found the cucumber and tomato salad and his favourite coriander chutney. He imagines her arranging it all on the plate and putting the plate on a tray to bring to him.

Now that it is too late, he has come to love her. Even if he could find some adequate language to tell her, she would dismiss him, would think he was trying to manipulate her, would think he was becoming sentimental as the old often do. She would never understand what it has taken for him to reach this point.

It doesn't matter. He loves her ignorance, her wide-ranging prejudices, her quick judgement of other people, her feelings of inadequacy, her suspicion of those who she feels are somehow 'better', her inability to follow a simple argument or even clear driving directions, her instinctive dislike of anything artistic, including art. He loves her sad walls of exclusion, including those that shut her out from anything that might demand a little understanding outside of the terrible moral code by which she attempts, and often fails, to live.

In the early mornings, while he is meant to be asleep, she sits in the least comfortable armchair near the gas fire, bent over her Bible. His belief is less regimented. His god, that bumbling, gentle, distracted librarian, is not the fire-breathing, vengeful Old Testament God. He is still amazed at her bottomless belief in all of it. She claims it is her refuge and her strength. Her lips move over the verses that spell out her failure in stark formulaic King James prose with its emphatic italics. Thou shalt *not*.

But she shall, she does, she cannot help herself. And worse than her voice raised against him, the words that ricochet out of her mouth, the fists clamped against her sides, is that sudden recognition, *I've done it again. I've done it again.* And she abruptly turns to the kitchen, to vent her despair on the clanging pans.

It is then he longs to tell her, *I know you're angry. It's all right to be angry.* She would not believe him. It isn't Christian to be angry. Even Christ, famously angry in the temple, got over it. Her anger has lasted all her life.

He can't move from the edge of the bed. He sits, leaning over the walker, his legs unresponsive.

Sunila comes in. 'I'm making some tea. Oh.' She stops. 'Let me help.' She puts her arm under his and eases him upright so that he can lean on the walker. Together, they shuffle to the armchair and she helps him sit, plumping the cushions behind him so that he is propped forward.

'Thank you, Sunila.'

'I'll bring your food, shall I?'

He smiles at her. 'Yes, please.' There is gentleness in his smile. He wants her to see that he loves her. He wants her to see that he understands how strong and generous she is. She just gets on with the next thing and the next. After they eat, she will clear away the dishes and wash them. She will help him back into bed. And tomorrow, she will go on, cleaning and washing and cooking and helping him write his letters and reading to him when he is too tired to read for himself.

And after, as he listens to her climbing the stairs, quietly closing the bedroom door, he will pray for her. Please give her the strength she needs so that she can keep on doing the next thing. And the next.

15

DYSPHAGIA: DIFFICULTY SWALLOWING

SEPTEMBER 2005

Nothing works any more. His hands, that used to function enough for him to lift a handkerchief to stem the eternal nasal drip, drip, can no longer push back the blanket to find the square of folded cotton. Some days his head feels too heavy to lift up.

He cannot even rock forwards and back to ease his sore back from the pressure of sitting in the same position in the same chair all day. The back of his head constantly itches. The nasal drip has turned into an embarrassing stream. He will not see visitors any more. He wishes to be left alone with his disgusting, defeated body. Is this his body's revenge on his younger, stronger, careless self?

Sunila and Tarani have been talking on the phone to Murad. The three-way phone conversation lasted a long time. They said *hospice*. Well, so be it. There was a time when he would have resisted. But what is the point of resisting? What power does he have, anyway? And does it really matter where he dies?

Perhaps it is better to lie in a bed, to be given mashed-up food, taken to the toilet and emptied, put back into the bed and left alone to lie there, staring at the ceiling. Maybe they will let him look out of a window. Maybe there will be a garden. Maybe the nurses will be kind, unlike the ones who were so cruel to Pavitra.

Pavitra. It has been a long time since he sat in front of her, trying to calm her terrible gasping for breath, unable even to reach forward and touch her poor thin hands. Was it last year? The year before? Anyway, she's gone now.

And he'll be next, after he's tucked away in some hospice where, they say, no one can hear you scream. He has heard the horror stories. *They wait until no one is looking and they twist your arms and pinch you where no one can see. They say that they even touch you on your privates.*

He clenches his eyes shut. Sunila will not allow it. She would never put him somewhere like that.

The living-room door squeaks open slowly and a dark-tufted head appears. Seven-year-old Sami. Arjun smiles and tries to articulate a greeting. Sami puts his finger on his lips.

'Ssh, Grandpa. You're too old for talking.'

Arjun smiles. 'No – one – is – too – old – for – talking.'

Sami seats himself carefully on a stool next to the chair, as though Arjun might be crushed by any sudden movement. Arjun supposes his grandson sees the decrepit wreck of a human being.

Sami says, 'I am very strong. You are very weak.'

'Yes – son.'

'I wrote a story about me. You can read it. ' He puts a crumpled piece of paper in Arjun's lap.

'Thank you – Sami.'

'I learned about the rainforest. There are all kinds of animals that stink. And there's a snake called a strictor that squeezes alligators.'

'Boa – constrictor.'

'No. A strictor. And then the snake lets go and the alligator is tired to death. Now I can sing you a song.'

Arjun nods. Sami clears his throat and slowly open his arms, takes a large breath, closes his eyes.

'Tarara *boom* de-ay. Tarara *boom* de-ay. Tarara *boom* de-ay. Tarara *boom* de-ay.' He lowers his arms and opens his eyes. 'The end. You can clap now.'

Arjun attempts to move his hands, but they lie like thin, exhausted birds in his lap. Sami reaches across, lifts his grandfather's hands and gently claps them together.

'Thank – you.'

'Mum knows the whole song.'

'Your – mother – is – a – good – singer.' It is something he has never told her. He is suddenly ashamed. He should have encouraged her to sing. Why didn't he? What held him back? Fear that she might be rejected by some snooty English person? Why didn't he insist on singing lessons?

'Mum's a *great* singer.' Sami rubs his forefinger across his nose. 'My nose is always scratchy after I sing.' He looks at his grandfather hopefully. 'I know more songs.'

'Sing – another.' Arjun is afraid of falling asleep and losing these few rare moments with his grandson.

Sami opens his arms again and closes his eyes and sings in a high-pitched voice, very fast. 'Singa-songa-sixpence-pocket-fulla-rye-four-an-twenty-blackbirds-baked-ina-pie.' He gasps and hauls in another great bucketful of air. 'When-the-pie-was-open-the-birds-beganta-sing-wazen-thata-dainty-dishta-set-before-the-king.'

Arjun smiles and nods. 'Beautiful, Sami.'

'I know a lot of songs. I can sing a bedtime song to help you sleep.'

He manages a breath. 'Yes.'

Sami stands with his arms straight by his sides. He tilts his head back, and with barely a breath between lines rattles off, 'Five little ducks went out one day, over the hill and far away. Mother Duck said quack, quack, quack, quack, but only four little ducks came back.'

Five little ducks. His mother, Jonti, Pavitra and he had come to England. His father had stayed behind, planning to earn money and send it on, but had died of pneumonia during the winter flooding. And now Mum, Jonti and Pavitra were also dead.

He was the eldest. He should have died first. But now he is hanging here on a cartoon thread as he slips from ledge to ledge; from walking, to shuffling, to leaning on a cane, a walker, to assisted walking, to a wheelchair. How long before he makes the last drop into the gulch?

Sami puts his hand on his grandfather's head. Arjun feels the weight and heat of the solid little hand. 'Now go to sleep.'

The tears slip out and trickle down Arjun's cheeks. He cannot lift his hand to wipe them away. Sami uses his t-shirt to wipe his grandfather's face. Arjun breathes in the little-boy sweat and a clean, young scent that might be laundry detergent. Arjun prefers to think of it as his grandson's special smell.

The living-room door opens again. Tarani comes in. 'Sami, let Grandpa rest.'

'I was singing to him.'

'That's lovely. Grandma has something in the kitchen for you.'

Sami says, 'But Grandpa is sad.'

Sunila would say, *He's just tired.* But Tarani says, 'Yes. He is sad.'

'Why?'

'Old people remember a lot of things and not all of them are happy.'

'Oh. When I grow up I'm only going to remember happy things so when I get old I won't be sad.'

'That's a good plan.'

Sami leaves and Tarani sits on the stool. 'Shall I plump up your pillows?'

Arjun shakes his head.

He tries. 'Tarani. I – am – so – sorry – about – your – singing.'

She sounds baffled. 'My singing?'

'We – should – have – sent – you – for – lessons.'

She starts to rub cream onto his hand. 'Well, I don't think I would have been much good. As long as Sami doesn't object to my singing.'

'He – is – so – proud – of – you. Me – too.'

He wants to tell her he should have listened to her long ago, encouraged her, told her how proud he was of her. He wants to tell her that she will be happy with this new man she's just met, whoever he is, that he will be better than the last one. Better than Arjun's marriage to Sunila. He doesn't have enough breath to say any of it.

'I know, Dad. It's okay.' She smiles at him. Hesitates. 'Sometimes I'm impatient with Sami. He is only being his curious little self. But I've got all these other things to do. You know, last week, we were going to Haseena Aunty's house. I had to drop him off and then pick up the dry-cleaning and do some photocopying. He was dawdling around and making me crazy. Then, just as we're finally there and walking up the drive, he looks up and sees the bushes. "Lavender, Mum!" You should have seen him, Dad. He pushed his face right into the bush and inhaled. I though the whole thing was going to disappear up his nose.' She laughs. 'Then he said, "You smell it, too." I was about to tell him to hurry up, but I did smell it. And it was like the breath of morning.'

Feels her taking his useless hands and placing them around her waist. Feels his daughter embrace him. There is some pain you cannot breathe through. She picks up the crumpled story. 'He was so excited to bring this to you.' She places it between Arjun's hands.

'Thank you, pet.' And closes his eyes, the grip on his grandson's story loosening.

I am seven yeers old. My hare is darkish. I am nice to athre popel. My hobbis are to paint and drwor I like to play baskitball. Oh and also my name is Sami. Reneber all the things that I do. Good by now I am done ritig.

ACKNOWLEDGEMENTS

Magnums of champagne or appropriate non-alcoholic beverage to:

Editors: John Reed who first believed in me, Jean Casella who nurtured the novel, Juliet Mabey, Charlotte Van Wijk and Holly Roberts, the amazingly patient and encouraging editors at Oneworld Publications.

Christopher Learned, Jerry Mansfield, Jeff Murphy, David Patnoe and Pamela West, who gave invaluable feedback in the novel's early stages.

The Flamingo Diamond Chix who are my Cheer-Group Ultima.

Ed Hunter for his email to Aliya Hunter.

My family in England.

My cousin Stephen for his joke about the Colosseum.

My dear friends Zena Fairweather, Kim Young and Helen Nathaniel.

My daughter, Aliya, for the gift of herself and the use of her childhood stories and sayings.

My patient and loving husband, Andy.